# Down East
## on Nelson Island

# Down East on Nelson Island

## Karen E. Dodd

Pentland Press, Inc.
www.pentlandpressusa.com

PUBLISHED BY PENTLAND, PRESS, INC.
5122 Bur Oak Circle, Raleigh, NC 27612
United States of America
919-782-0281

ISBN: 1-57197-314-1
Library of Congress Control Number: 2001 135829
Printed in the United States of America

# PREFACE

Nelson Island and all its characters exist in my mind. I suppose if I could chop off a piece of Open Ground Farm in Carteret County and plop it down in Core Sound somewhere east of Beaufort, NC, near Harkers Island, that's where it would be. The story and events sound like something that may have happened to me, my family and friends. I grew up on the coast and have been around boats all my life. I hope you enjoy my imagined island and all its imagined characters.

# ACKNOWLEDGMENTS

I'd like to acknowledge my dear husband, Denton, who patiently waits for me to leave the computer each writing day. I am grateful for Roy Styron, David McFadyen, D.A., Dr. Bill Ramseur and Carteret County General Hospital for answering my questions. My thanks and love go to Christine Grotheer, my daughter, and Rachel Grotheer, my granddaughter. I have a sister, Sarah Leary, and niece, Jennifer Kale, who inspired a few exciting moments of the story. I thank my parents, Sam and Sarah Kale, who gave me a lifetime of coastal memories. Last and certainly not least I want to mention my older sister, Pat Phillips. When we were young, she had a doll she named Picklepuss.

# Nelson Island

Arthur Austin slid his feet into a pair of scuffed deck shoes. While the coffee brewed he fixed a bowl of cereal then fed and watered the cat. He paused to inhale the salt air. Shielding his eyes, he looked over the marshland to the east. He'd weeded the flower bed and cut the grass the previous day. A faint odor of green onions still clung to the air. The twisted water oaks stretched out over the picket fence that was already full of red roses in late May. He ran his hand over the few remaining hairs on his head. "Well, Wobbles, we're going to get some company today. I expect you to be on your best behavior. I have my doubts about whether we can carry this off. With your help and the Lord's above, we can do it. If not, we'll worry about it later when it gets here, okay?" He scratched the cat's neck and then agilely stood to watch his friend.

"Morning, Arthur." A short portly man panted up his drive on an old bicycle. He wolf whistled, "You sure look handsome this morning. Where'd you get that pretty pink shirt?"

Arthur turned back inside his door, "Hey Smitty, my daughter Louise sent me this shirt. I think Rachel helped her pick it out so I thought I'd wear it today. It might help with my first impression on the girl. Come in for a cup of coffee. I'm afraid that's all I have to offer you this morning. That and a bowl of cereal."

"You know how Margaret gets on me about my weight," Smitty sighed as he tugged his trousers up. "Nothing to eat. I guess I better settle for a cup of coffee if you could spare it." He eyed the sugar bowl and peered into the refrigerator looking for a can of milk. Finding none, Smitty went to the pantry, selected a small can from the shelf and shuffled back into the kitchen. Arthur had already placed the church key on the counter alongside a coffee mug. Smitty dipped two heaping spoons of sugar into the mug and added the milk before topping the cup off with coffee.

"What time you reckon they'll be getting here?" He slurped the coffee between his lips, while reaching over to grab a few strawberries.

"Oh, they should be eating now. You know I never could get used to all that silverware and formal eating. Someone was always watching from the kitchen door to bring anything that was needed. There's probably a platter of eggs, a bowl of grits, and depending on my former wife's whim, fresh sausage, bacon or liver mush." Arthur watched as Smitty's tongue licked his top lip imagining the breakfast three hundred miles away.

"I suppose they'll be on the road by nine and pulling into my yard within seven or eight hours. They'll probably come through Raleigh and down Highway 70. Barring any traffic delays, they'll be here in time for supper," Arthur answered. "I've gotta get to the store and pick up a few things. Care to go with me?"

His friend finished off the last strawberry, pulled the business section from the paper and proceeded to go over the stock page, squinting at the small print. "Hmmm, eh, no thanks. I'm supposed to be on my bike now, sweating off the pounds. Margaret has set me up a regimen of diet and thirty minutes of bike riding, but I'll stay here until you're ready to leave and walk you to that pink topless truck of yours." Smitty grinned, having taken a good-natured stab at Arthur's current vehicle. He continued staring at the paper. He, in fact, was responsible for the truck's name, the Pink Panther.

Arthur finished breakfast cleanup and his morning toilet while his friend read the paper. Grabbing his cap from the wall rack, he helped Smitty through the screened door. "Care to sneak over for dessert and coffee this evening, Smitty? We should be finishing up about seven." As he pulled his long, thin legs into the cab and shut the door, he grinned at his friend bike-wobbling down his drive.

"Sounds good, I'll try to make it." Smitty barely cleared the fence post and turned up the road waving one hand.

"That bike will be the end of you yet, Smitty!" Arthur waved at his disappearing friend.

On the way to town, Arthur reviewed the recent events that led to hosting an eight-year-old girl for the summer. He enjoyed the brief visits from his daughter when she was growing up, but it came as a surprise when she called to ask if the granddaughter, Rachel, could spend the summer. Rachel's parents, Louise and Ron, were traveling to China and Australia for the summer, a combination pleasure and business trip. The psychology class Louise had recently taken exposed the distance between her family and her father. She hoped this gesture of good faith would lessen the gap between the two homes.

He received Christmas and birthday greetings in the past but hadn't met his little visitor in person. He kept a family snapshot in his wallet and the framed picture on the bureau in his bedroom.

He remembered a conversation he had with Sarah Styron, when they first began dating.

"My wife, Coral, never remarried. The family lawyer quietly handled our divorce. I guess I opted for an easier life without the career and social pressure that was designed for me by my in-laws. I saw my daughter on her beach jaunts with her school friends. I hadn't seen my wife until Louise's wedding." He chuckled as he remembered one episode in particular, "The first time I met Coral's parents, she had dragged me to a family reunion. We both were still attending college. My tight seersucker suit wilted in the summer heat. I felt like a hard crab on a grassy lawn—out of place. 'So what do you do, Arthur, down on your beach?' Those folks sure wanted to know what I did. 'I work for the town during the summer,' was all I said. Then this sweet young thing sidled up to me while Coral had wandered off. She asked the same thing, leaning at me in a skin-tight dress with a very low neckline.

"I had all I could take that day. I said, 'I'm the sanitation engineer for the town.' 'Ooh,' she said and ran a finger up my arm and tickled my chin. 'What does a sanitation engineer do at the beach?' 'My buddy drives the truck and I walk beside it. As we get to each house I pick up the trash can and dump it into the truck.' She glared at me, made an excuse and hurried off.

"Coral never returned my calls or letters after I left her. My mamma had died then, so I came back and lived here with my daddy. The Marine Corps Air Station hired me immediately. My civil service job allowed me time to do what I enjoy: working on boats, fishing, crabbing and watching the sun come up every morning over that marsh. I like being alone, Sarah, but I enjoy being with you too." Sarah had understood. The same undertow had brought her back to the island after her husband died.

He wondered what kind of summer he had ahead as he pulled his truck, the Pink Panther, into a Sarah's side parking lot. Pushing open the door to the combination bakery and gift shop, Arthur smelled the bread already baking in the big ovens behind the counter. Warm cinnamon buns and pecan stickies were under the glass case, as well as brownies and chocolate chip cookies. Sarah was talking to Belle Nelson, the island curiosity. Belle was widowed by a fishing boat accident. She roamed the island picking up driftwood and bits of trash, eventually shaping them into wall hangings, wind chimes and other sea island treasures that tourists enjoyed buying. She wore shapeless men's trousers held up by old neckties tied at the waist and multiple layered shirts which she found at yard sales and thrift shops. On her feet was the ever-present pair of thick socks and her Birkenstock sandals.

Sarah's shop was one of the primary sellers for her creations. Arthur knew some of the island kids played pranks on Belle. She developed a defensive ranting that she dished out appropriately when provoked. As a result some islanders called her crazy. Arthur admired her independence and her energy.

He waited until the two women finished their business and held the door open for the departing Belle. Talking to herself, the woman stooped to lift the handle of her red wagon on the sidewalk and tromped down the street.

"Morning, Sarah, looked like big business going on there," Arthur nodded at the departing woman.

"Oh, poor Belle. Social Services came out to check on her this week." Sarah took a swallow from her third cup of coffee. "You know she takes care of her granddaughter since her daughter ran off. Someone made a complaint that the child wasn't getting proper care. Humph. There is more love in that woman than meets the eye. You should hear her talk about Pammy Lee. People should mind their own business. That's what I say. I wonder if there's anything that we can do to help." Sarah's face colored with argument. Arthur noted Sarah didn't follow her own advice. "What do you think? Pammy Lee is about the age of your granddaughter. How would you feel if you were raising that child and someone came in investigating your child-rearing habits? That woman had the audacity to ask if Belle was the legal guardian of the child. Since when does a judge have say so in if it's right for her grandmamma to have her?" Sarah paused a moment, caught up in her need to assist. "I'm sorry, Arthur. I can't help myself. I've got to do something. I'll chew on the matter later. Now about your granddaughter . . ."

Trying to change Sarah's mind about getting the "we" involved in someone else's problem was like trying to change the tides. He took a different tack. "What kind of pies do we have, my dear?" He leaned over the counter and grinned up at her.

Pushing a misplaced graying bang from her forehead, she squatted behind the viewing case and pointed. "Oh, I made a strawberry and a cherry pie but you must get this delightful coconut cake with the seven minute frosting." Over the years he and Sarah had shared evening meals, conversations, arguments, and many sunsets. Islanders gossiped she was his "girl." "When are you going to bring that grandyoungun over for me to meet?"

He looked into her green eyes. "First thing tomorrow morning. They won't be in until tonight, after supper'll be too late. I'm praying there won't be much of a problem for us to get to know each other." He hesitated thinking about the task ahead, once again. Was he doing the right thing? He was a man of few words and quick judgments, often lacking patience.

"There's nothing for you to be worried about. She'll love you and all the things you're going to do together. She's what you need to round off those rough corners you've been developing over the years, Arthur Austin. I'm not complaining, mind you, but you've gotten too set in your ways. It'll add a little spice to your life having a child around." Sarah smiled into the twinkling eyes she had grown to love over the past few years.

Arthur, known as a quiet man on the island, rarely involved himself in politics or gossip. He shaved when he felt like it, grew or caught most of his food. He kept to himself. Sarah dropped the cake in a cardboard box and bagged some cookies. "Yep, you'll do fine by her." Arthur paid for his purchases and gave her a kiss on her cheek, smelling the fragrance of her short hair and coffee breath. He left to continue his morning chores.

He drove a few blocks down the street to the local grocery store. After shopping he loaded all his purchases into the back of the truck and made one last stop at the fish house. He stepped over the melted ice puddles and scanned the bins of fish peeking out from under their icy blankets. The smell of fresh-caught seafood hung in the cool air. "Give me a couple of pounds of these shrimp and dress that yellow fin, Billy." Arthur looked about the old fish house. "There aren't many of these left. Now most people buy their seafood at supermarkets or roadside vendors." He watched the man prepare the fish. "Billy, I'm going to bring my granddaughter down here and show her around before that son of yours replaces this with a video store or a pizza parlor."

"Ya' dew that very thing, Arthur. Oi'll be here to shew her around." Nelson Island people had a unique way of talking that created two syllables out of one and changed vowels. The old fish man chuckled, displaying a toothless grin. He wrapped the seafood in white waxed paper, tying it with a string. "If yer not goin' ro'ight home I ken scoop some ice in a bag fer ya' ta put that fish on."

Arthur shook his head, "No thanks, I'm heading straight home now." He collected his change and carried his seafood out to the truck.

# The Introduction

Later, Arthur sat on the porch rocker with his bare feet propped up on the railing. He couldn't doze; he was too excited. The fish and the now-peeled shrimp were chilling in the refrigerator. He'd made a salad and washed and capped another quart of strawberries from the garden. Arthur's cat hopped up into his lap. She purred under his touch. "I guess we're ready, girl. My stomach is a might queasy. Maybe chamomile will settle it down."

In the distance a church bell struck the hour. Arthur glanced once more about the porch and yard. He went back inside to fix a cup of tea.

The shiny sports utility vehicle pulled into the yard before he'd finished brewing the tea. Arthur left the cup sitting on the counter as he hurried through the screened door. He went out, hugged his daughter and shook his son-in-law's hand. Then he stared at the red-haired girl eyeing him, his small house with the shell walk and—his cat.

"Daddy, I hope this isn't too much trouble for you. I realize Rachel could have stayed with Mamma, but I wanted her to get to know you. She'll go to bed when you tell her. She can take her own bath and dress herself. Mary, our housekeeper, usually fixes her an afternoon snack if she gets hungry. She likes to read. Rachel can show you her doll and paints. She won't be any trouble at all. I usually have Mary pick her up from school and she's polite. You mind that she says 'sir' and 'ma'am.' She's smart too, Daddy. I know she's ahead of most children her age in school. She attends a private school, you know. Rachel even wears a uniform, don't you honey?" Louise rattled on.

Rachel stood in her pink dress, lace socks and white patent leather shoes. Her knapsack of favorite things hung from one hand. The long French braid that was so carefully pulled up that morning was now falling from the barrettes. While her parents were unloading the bags from the car Arthur picked up the cat and sat on the edge of the front steps. "Rachel, would you like to meet Wobbles?" He placed the cat on his legs and began stroking its head. The girl stepped to the porch and tentatively put out her hand.

"Will she scratch me? There's a mean cat at Grandmother's that likes to scratch me."

"I don't think so. She's a pretty good old cat. She likes to be petted. Can't you hear her purring?"

"Well isn't that nice, Rachel, you've made a friend. Daddy, has that old cat had all her shots? I don't want Rachel to catch ringworm or anything while she's visiting." Rachel, looking up to her mother, quickly pulled her hand back.

"I'm sure this old cat doesn't have anything I don't have, and quit scaring your daughter before she has a chance to get to know me and my cat here."

His daughter made a face like his former wife's. "Dad, I hate to drop Rachel here and run but we must get back to the Raleigh airport tonight. Our flight's been changed."

Arthur's face displayed a mild shock. "Good-bye, sweetheart. Give Mamma a hug and then give Daddy a hug and a kiss." The girl complied. The SUV honked, then backed from the yard.

Rachel waved and then turned to the man. "Grandfather, I have to go to the bathroom."

"Come on in and I'll show you where it's at."

Rachel sat on the commode lid, holding her face in her hands. She felt a huge hole in her chest just beneath her throat. "I'm not going to cry. I'm not going to cry. I won't cry." She stood facing the oval mirror that hung over the sink. She lathered the small bar of soap. Leaning over, so as not to get the front of her dress wet, she soaped her face and hands carefully. "Why couldn't I go with Mamma and Daddy? I wouldn't be any trouble. I'd be good. They wouldn't have to worry about me . . ." She walked to the window. The short-cropped grass went down to the water's edge where a dock was built. She looked at the blue and white boat. "Is that his boat? There's a big bird in the marsh. Grandfather looks like a grouch, but maybe not. Maybe I'll like him. Mamma said I'd like it here. Maybe it won't be so bad. I hope his old cat will like me!" She turned once more to check her face in the mirror. She pictured in her mind her mother doing the same thing when she was here as a girl. "Maybe she used the same bar of soap. She could have used these same rose-colored towels. Oh well." With that thought in mind, she opened the door and went to find her grandfather.

He was sitting on her bed beside her bags. Arthur helped Rachel unpack her suitcases. He noticed a lot of frilly dresses but few play clothes. He didn't say anything. She'd emptied her backpack on the bed. Books, paintbrushes and a paint palette, a well-worn bit of blanket edge and a cloth doll fell from the bag. Arthur stifled a cough. Thirty-three years ago when he'd learned he was a father he'd purchased the doll in New Bern. "What's this?" he asked.

"Mamma named her Picklepuss. I found her in an old toy box in the attic," Rachel said. The small cloth doll had big blue eyes and red yarn hair pulled back in pigtails. Socks at the ankle turned down over the Mary Jane shoes painted on her feet. A blouse-petticoat peeked out from under a plaid jumper. Large pink lips puckered a kiss or a pout depending on the doll's mood. Staring at it now, Arthur wondered what the doll had seen and heard in the past thirty years.

"Grandmother says I'm getting too old for dolls, but I thought I'd bring her, in case I get lonely." She gathered the doll in her arms, taking Arthur's hand. They went downstairs, Arthur making sure he didn't hit his head on the low overhang above the steps.

Rachel looked about the large open room that was to be her home for the summer. An old spread was pulled over the couch; a recliner and a lamp sat in the corner. There was a stack of magazines and papers beside the chair. A sisal rug covered the floor. The curtains hadn't been changed in years.

Too many rainy afternoons of open windows left yellow watermark stains. A local artist's painting hung on one varnished pine wall. The room had once been two rooms, but when his father died Arthur had removed the dividing wall and opened the kitchen and living room into one space. He lengthened the porch and enclosed one portion that allowed him to add a bathroom upstairs and enlarge his own bath downstairs.

Despite her first impression, Rachel felt comfortable as she pulled out a chair by the table, and fiddled with the place mat while Arthur began the meal. "Do you like shrimp and fish?" Arthur tried to put a little enthusiasm in his voice. "Come here and help me if you don't mind."

"I've never cooked anything before. Grandfather, are you sure you want my help?"

"Here, you better tie this around you." Arthur tugged a dishtowel from the stove handle. "I don't want you to mess up that pretty dress. First we put water in the pot and some seasoning and then turn on the burner. When you see little bubbles around the edge of the pan let me know. Now these shrimp will turn pink as they cook." He pulled a stool up to the counter and placed the bowl of cold peeled shrimp in front of her.

"While we wait, how about getting those salads from the refrigerator and finish setting the table?" He pointed out where to find silverware and napkins. By the time she finished setting the table she was pleased with herself. Arthur lifted her up to the stool and pushed her hand into the bowl of cold, slimy shrimp.

"I'd like you to add these to the water and then let me know when they turn pink, okay?" He went to light the propane grill, returning to find Rachel squishing her hands through the bowl of cold shrimp. She enjoyed the feel of the soft, cool peeled creatures and forgot her recent abandonment. "Here, here, let me show you how to do it." She looked up, startled by his voice. He made a mental note not to sound so gruff in the future. Arthur took her hand and dropped a handful of shrimp into the simmering water. He watched as she repeated the task. Rachel wiped her hands and watched as the shrimp began cooking.

"I've seen shrimp cocktails at restaurants but never knew this is how they looked before they cooked," Rachel exclaimed. Arthur returned to the grill with the plate of tuna when she called, "Grandfather, they're turning pink!" Arthur kept an eye back in the kitchen while turning the tuna on the grill. Rachel stood on the stool, peering into the pot, stirring with a wooden spoon. Arthur smiled, acknowledging her newfound confidence.

"When *all of them* are pink, give me another holler, Picklepuss."

She giggled, "I'm not Picklepuss." Arthur went outside, brushed the chunk of meat with marinade, then peered back. When the meal was ready they sat together at the table. Arthur said grace holding her hand. They ate their meal slowly, getting acquainted with one another. "I like to read and draw and color and paint. I'll make you some pictures, Grandfather."

"We'll have to make sure you get to see the bookmobile when it comes to the island. I like to fish. I grow my own tomatoes and vegetables in the garden. I also like to walk the beach. Would you like to do those kinds of things?" She ate more than Arthur expected for the first night, favoring the shrimp over the tuna. He figured the leftover tuna would make a nice salad for the next day. They were clearing the dishes when there was a tap at the door.

Rachel sat politely while Smitty told about his day's activities and jabbered on about sports. Arthur wondered which of the newcomers was the more uncomfortable. One talked from nervousness; the other sat and watched quietly as the cake and coffee were consumed. They sat on the porch, the southwest breeze keeping the mosquitoes and no-see-ums away.

Rachel stroked the cat, listening to the men talk. Crickets and a marsh hen called from the dark. Fireflies danced among the bushes. Yawning, she went upstairs. She experimented with the shower, bathed and changed into her pajamas. When Arthur went to check on Rachel, she was asleep, Picklepuss snuggled to her face. He stared at the doll clutched in her hand. "Good night Picklepuss," he spoke gently before returning to his friend below.

# Granddaughter Day Two

Arthur heard Rachel creep down the steps. He looked up to see her first smile of the day. "Good morning, Grandfather."

"Well good morning Picklepuss, and you too, Rachel. Let's decide right now what you'll call me. I'm not too fond of Grandfather, too fussy for me."

"Hmmm, Grandpop? Pa-Pa? I know, how about Grandpa?" Rachel smiled after considering the options.

"Perfect," Arthur said, "I was feeling too formal with the Grandfather name." A breeze smelling of marsh grass ruffled out the curtains. "What do you want for breakfast? I have eggs and bacon, pancakes, or we can go out for something. You decide." Rachel looked at him with curiosity. She'd never been asked what she wanted for breakfast before.

"Scrambled eggs and bacon, I think." Then she hurried upstairs to change. Arthur began frying the bacon in a large iron skillet. Rachel changed into a plaid jumper and arrived at Arthur's elbow as he was putting the bacon on paper towels.

"Put Picklepuss down. Here, put on your apron. I need help with the toast." She climbed on the stool to reach the counter better. While he cracked the eggs into the mixing bowl she laid the bread out, spreading each piece with a pat of butter. "Tell me when it turns brown. Both eggs and toast should be done about the same time." Arthur poured the eggs into the hot bacon grease. He pushed the tray into the broiler. Rachel squinched up her nose, watching the raw eggs swirl in the grease.

Seated at the table, she hesitated before eating the brown-colored eggs, but after her first bite said, "Mmm, this is not bad." Spreading the toast with jam, she realized she was hungry. Quickly finishing the meal, she asked, "What will we do now, Granfa—, I mean, Grandpa?"

Looking at her fallen braid Arthur asked, "How about helping me learn how to fix your hair? It looks like a two-person chore." Rachel went upstairs, returning with brush, hair clips and elastic bands. She sat on the hassock. He separated the long strands, taking care not to pull too hard. "Do you want to go to the beach today? Maybe we can swim if the jellyfish aren't too bad. I bet you can find some nice shells to take home. We'll have a picnic."

Rachel's eyes lit up, "Absolutely!" Being with Grandpa was going to be fun. Her mother was right.

"Did you bring a bathing suit and shorts?" He emptied his coffee mug with one long swallow.

Rachel's eyebrows went up, "Oh no, Grandpa." Her hand unconsciously reached for the doll and drew it to her face.

"Never mind," he said. "We can pick up a few things at my church's consignment shop." He finished with her hair and together they started clearing the breakfast dishes.

✿✿✿

"Morning, Miss Jean, this is Rachel. Jean, my grand-daughter needs some clothes to wear on the boat and around the island this summer."

Jean eyed the youngster and took her over to a rack of play clothes. There were four sets of twins on the island, a bit older than Rachel. Their parents competed to have the cutest dressed set of twins in school. Outgrown clothes were often recycled through the church consignment shop. She selected several pairs of shorts, tee shirts, a couple of pairs of jeans, a red zip jersey jacket, and a pair of plastic gooey shoes called "jellies." Rachel picked through the pile, holding up a few. Changing behind a curtain she reappeared. "Ta-Dah!" Rachel grinned, showing off her new clothes.

"Make sure you bring her to church this Sunday, Arthur. She'll meet a lot of other children. Will she be here long enough to attend the children's Vacation Bible School we're having at the end of summer? Barbara Moore would love to include her in the activities."

Pausing momentarily to remember the forceful director of children's programs, he responded, "Yep, we'll be in church. We have plans to be together all summer, don't we, Rachel?" Rachel bobbed up and down trying the feel of the new sandals. While paying for his purchases, Arthur watched his granddaughter walk through the door and out to the truck.

"I know Barbara can be tiresome at times, Arthur, but she is really doing wonderful things with the children." Jean found the woman who had moved down to the island from Connecticut to be pushy and too vocal at times. She shrugged her shoulders and smirked off the memory of the way Barbara had aimed herself at Arthur. When it came to

19

Miss Barbara, she seemed to stick like super glue on any available man in the area. "I think she had her eye on you one time. Good thing Bitsy Parker straightened her out about you and Sarah." Ignoring the last remark, Arthur tipped his cap and departed the store.

"I like your pink truck, Grandpa. It's a cool color and I like the bounce when we go over a bump." Rachel pulled the seat belt around her waist. "How come you have a pink truck without a roof, Grandpa?" She twiddled her new shoes together as Arthur placed the bag full of 'new old' clothes on the floor between them.

Arthur eased his frame behind the wheel and explained, "I was going to the Maritime Museum. That's in Beaufort, another place we're going to visit. I spied the truck on Front Street with a For Sale sign. I'm not too particular about what I drive and the price was right. A Beaufort boy wanted a motorcycle and needed cash. He'd chopped off the top of the cab and painted it this Pepto Bismol pink. When we found the decapitated top under his Mamma's porch, he helped me load it. I don't mind the Grateful Dead stickers, but the low rider chassis barely clears the center hump in my drive." He chuckled, remembering, "It seems to have caused quite a scandal here. You should have seen the stares I got that first day. I guess people have gotten used to it, and me, by now. All I get these days are smiles and waves." Arthur had refastened the cab top to the chassis with large hinges. For winter driving, he tipped the roof up, sealing it off with duct tape. It met his needs.

As they drove along the island road, Rachel noticed drivers waving their hands as they approached. "Do you know everybody who lives here?" she asked as she watched him lift a hand to another car.

"Well, yes and no. Most folks who live on the island have been here a while. It's a polite courtesy, see, to wave at one another as we meet. I've never thought about it. Done it all my life, like my daddy did before me."

"I can't imagine Grandmother waving at everybody in Charlotte. She knows a lot of people, but she doesn't wave like you do." Rachel sat back in her seat, rubbing her hand against the back of her head. "Can I try it too?"

"Sure, here comes a truck now, let's both wave." She giggled as the people in the approaching vehicle returned their waves. Even the dog in back barked. "That, there on the road ahead, is Miss Belle and her granddaughter, Pammy Lee." He raised his palm at the woman who looked down as they passed, but the copper-skinned child waved back, smiling. "Well sometimes not everyone waves. Hey, I have someone I want you to meet. She's my special lady friend. She runs her own business, a bakery and gift shop. I hope you like her." Arthur pulled the truck up in front of Sarah's and opened the screened door. Rachel felt like jumping in her new shoes. The new "jellies" squished as she landed.

"Mmmmm, I think I'm going to like coming here," Rachel murmured as her nose sniffed in the early morning bakery smells. She glanced into the glass case, eyeing the gingerbread and sugar cookies as a tall woman wiped her hands and came forward from the back of the store.

"Lord 'a mercy, well you must be Rachel. Aren't you a pretty thing? Where did you get that red hair? Arthur, did you ever have red hair before I met you?" Sarah's eyebrows went up as she glanced at Rachel's faded pink shirt, blue jean shorts and purple shoes.

"We just came from the consignment store and bought some new togs. What do you think?" Arthur asked.

Sarah stepped back, her hands on her hips, and surveyed the pair. She shook her head, smiling. "Aren't you the cat's meow? You look special in those clothes and I'm in the mood for a little party for the occasion. How about we sit down over there and if no one comes in for a few minutes we can have milk and a cookie?" She refilled her large coffee mug. "Honey, you want chocolate or white milk?"

Both Rachel and her grandfather answered together, "Chocolate." They laughed as they carried their snack to the table.

"Well, now I want to know all about you, Rachel. What grade are you in? What's your favorite class in school? I used to teach the fourth grade." Munching their cookies and sipping from cartons of milk, they eyed each other. Rachel wiped the chocolate mustache from her mouth with a napkin carefully pulled from the box on the table. She politely answered all of Sarah's questions.

"I'm almost nine years old. I'll be in the third grade. I like geography and art class best. I have a question too." She looked over to her grandfather. "Grandpa, are you going to marry Miss Sarah? I like her a lot."

Sarah recovered first from the question. "Well, Rachel, he has never asked me, but if he does, I'll tell you first." When embarrassed, his high forehead looked like a glowing red bulb. Arthur covered his mouth as he coughed into a dinette napkin, his face returning to its normal color.

"May I be excused?" Arthur choked down his last bite of cookie and pulled Rachel's chair back as she stood.

"Do you want to go outside and wait for me?" Arthur asked Rachel.

While the couple cleaned up, she wandered out the door and looked down the street. "This isn't a big town like Charlotte, for sure," she said to herself. The wind-shaped oak and cedar trees cloaked the street, shading the sidewalk along storefronts. There was a bank at the corner where another street cut across the main street at an angle. She supposed living on an island didn't allow for a very wide town. Up the street walked a boy and a girl with a big black dog between them. Further behind she saw the lady called Belle and her granddaughter, Pammy Lee. The closer pair had dark short hair, cut identically with bangs dropping above their eyebrows. They wore matching Carolina tee shirts and cut-off jeans.

They stopped a few steps away from her, "Who're you? I've never seen you around," asked the boy. Rachel was learning island folks speak their mind easily.

"I'm Rachel Grady and I'm here with my grandpa," she said, pointing back into the store. They stood on their toes and looked inside at the couple cleaning off the table. The boy wiped his bangs off his forehead with one hand as he rubbed the big dog's ear with the other. The dog looked too, then slobbered his tongue across the boy's sun-browned hand. He wiped his hand unconsciously on his pants then stuck it out to Rachel, introducing himself and the girl.

"I'm Jesse and this is Jewel. We're twins. We live not far from Mr. Arthur. I guess we'll see you around. Mamma's waiting or we'd stay to talk a bit." He nudged the dog along with his knee. His sister, Jewel, lifted a hand and waved good-bye as they headed down the street.

Arthur came out of the bakery and stared after the two children, black dog between them, ambling toward the grocery. He recognized them as the Garner twins who lived a few houses from him. "So you've met folks your own age—good. It doesn't take you long to make friends. That's easy to see." Rachel smiled up to her grandfather, grasped his hand, and hopped on one foot all the way to the truck.

When they pulled into his yard, Wobbles came to greet them. Rachel stooped and ran her hand across the cat's back. They unloaded their purchases. Stopping briefly in the house to pack a few things, Arthur walked his granddaughter to the backyard where his 27-foot Albin trawler was docked.

# Miss Belle

"Pull out a chair, Belle, and sit a spell." Sarah came around the counter. She brought them both fresh cups of coffee. "Honey, would you like a cookie? I have a broken gingerbread boy back there that you can have." She pointed Pammy Lee to the back counter, then pulled out her own chair.

"Me-maw, may I have a cookie? I'd rather go outside and eat, if that's okay." Her grandmother nodded and waved the child out the door. Sarah watched the blue-eyed, darkskinned child select a cookie and leave.

"Oh, Sarah, what am I going to do? I don't know what I'll do if they say I can't keep Pammy Lee. Who would take her? I know a mixed-race child can be confused by their color but family is important. And I am her family, or all she has now.

"I s'wan when her mother told me she was pregnant with a black boy's child, I all but threw her out of the house. But when that child was born, right then I knew that I wouldn't deny her. When I saw her that first time something swelled in my heart. She's my blood. I wanted to hold her and have never stopped loving her. I have no idea where her Mamma is now. She hasn't phoned in months. She was waiting tables in Greensboro the last I heard but she said she was taking some college classes. That's good isn't it? I don't know if she'll ever get straight and come back home. Sarah, what am I gonna do?"

Looking into Belle's tearing pale blue eyes, Sarah drew Belle's hands across the table and squeezed them tight. "We have to have a plan. Now tell me what that woman had to say when she came out. Then perhaps, I need to come out to your place and offer some suggestions about fixing it up if that's what they want. I need to know everything, Belle, or I won't be able to help."

"Well, first I have to say I brung it on myself. There's some mean boys on this island and they're always taunting me and teasing Pammy Lee in school. I don't care what they say about me but they better not mess with my grand-child.

"We were out on the Western Shore two weeks back. I like to find those small cockleshells to make the mirrors and picture frames that sell so well. We had a big bag full when we found some oyster rock that had washed up—all bleached by the sun. Pretty stuff. My mind was in its cre-ative mode. I didn't even hear them tearing out of the woods until they were right on us. Riding those three- and four-wheel 'all terrain vehicles.' Lord, honey, they came screaming down on us and circled about us and were hol-lering bad language. I rose up and threw a hex on them. You know like they do in the movies? I started doing this crazy arm waving stuff. Well you wouldn't believe it. Like an answered prayer, one wheel got stuck in another wheel and two of 'em flipped over right there. As if I did it myself with the curse. I grabbed up Pammy Lee and we lit out of there fast.

"You know I don't know nothing about such stuff, Sarah. We go to the same church you do. I'm one of the Lord's own. I may dress a bit different." Under her breath she went on, "I wear long sleeves and old pants to avoid the sun. And when I get a'painting I mess up my clothes so these ole clothes work for me. People pay me never yew mind and that's what I want.

"And as for where we live, well, you know that abandoned fish factory we bought thirty years ago has been my home ever since I was married. We jest live a bit different but who's to say one's ways are right and another's wrong? Well one o' those boy's mothers, Miss High and Mighty, calls the sheriff, Social Services, and every county agency in the book trying to get back at me. I don't think those boys had a sprained ankle between them." Belle hadn't confided this much to another person in years. She poured her story out into her friend's ample lap.

Sarah knew where Belle lived on the eastern end of the island. Fifty years before, there had been a menhaden fish factory there but the fish and interest in menhaden had long gone. Belle's husband had an idea to buy the property, fixing it up as time allowed. Since his death, Belle had boarded-up space and knocked out rooms to suit her needs and the living requirements for her daughter, son, and now, her granddaughter.

Sarah hadn't visited in years but remembered a jumble of wood and collected trash. Old floats and driftwood hung from the ceilings at odd angles in fascinating shapes. Often referred to as "green box" vintage, the home was furnished by what the woman had found in the county trash boxes and curbside castoffs. Their dining room table was a large discarded cable spool. Assorted chairs were either recovered or painted. The kitchen and bath was fortunately plumbed before Harold's death. Belle had collected cans of paint from construction sites and trash bins. She painted walls with bright colorful shore scenes and imaginary sea creatures.

"Let me do some phone calling, Belle. I'll find out, if I can, how much trouble you're in. I have a friend that works at Social Services. I'll see if she can tell me anything." Sarah looked up to see Pammy Lee looking in the window, her nose against the glass. "You have a child to get home. I'll talk to you later this week, alright? Uh, Belle, are you okay financially? I have to pry. Do you have enough money for clothes and food and such?"

Belle snorted, "Lord, honey, I wish that was the problem! When Harold died we had all these little accidental death double indemnity policies. I had to find myself a financial planner to help me invest all the money. No, Sarah, we got plenty of money. I can't even use up all the income it makes each year.

"Now you don't go telling this to anybody. That child has never needed anything I couldn't afford. When I die Harold Jr., Brenda Lee, if I ever find her, and Pammy Lee will be well provided for. That money has been growing for over twenty-five years now."

Sarah breathed a sigh of relief for her friend's good financial fortune. She helped Belle collect her bag and hat. Belle reached over, hugged her friend and ambled out the door. Sarah's mind began to twirl.

# Cape Lookout

Arthur stopped and pointed to the boat's stern. "I named this boat for your mamma, Rachel. She's christened the *Lady Lou*." She studied the blue letters on the boat's backside. He threw the line in, lifted in a cooler of drinks and sandwich fixin's, and held her hand as she jumped aboard. He pointed her to the port side of the boat and a high seat that allowed her to see out. He warmed the engine, checked the bilge, and settled their change of clothes, food, hats, and suntan lotion in the aft cabin. She bounced Picklepuss in her lap as she waited.

"We're going to the beach in a boat, Grandpa?" her eyes opened wide at the question. She tucked Picklepuss beside her in her seat as Arthur searched through the pile of life jackets. He found one for her and nodded for her to slip her arms through the holes. He pulled the buckle-snap tight. She turned her nose up at the musty smell. Unless she sat high in her seat, the jacket neck rose above her nose. She tugged it down and sat back as he pushed the throttle forward and edged away from his dock. The noise of the engine seemed loud at first.

Rachel dozed off in the sun. She woke up as her head banged against the window.

Arthur reached over to slide the glass. "Let's open this so you can feel the breeze." He didn't want a seasick child on his hands. "That's Cape Lookout," he said, pointing at the diamond-painted lighthouse on the horizon. She fixed her eyes on the tower.

Arthur frowned as Tar Boy's black and red crab pot-laden boat cut across his bow. He lifted a hand in acknowledgment.

"Do you know him, Grandpa?" Rachel squinted over the water at the retreating boat.

Arthur nodded. "Tar Boy earned his name when he worked as a teenager with a local roofing company." Arthur had seen him often at the fish house or shuffling along the street. He remained a hard-muscled, dark-haired boy. For some reason, the man's mind hadn't grown with his body. He had a lazy eye that wandered as he talked. His yellow teeth and hacking cough betrayed his three-pack-a-day cigarette habit.

"Tar Boy was never any good with schoolwork but he knows how to hustle when there's money to be made. He shouldn't have waked us like that. Hold on to your seat good, Rachel. We're in for a rocking." Arthur turned the boat to ride across the man's waves. He heard that occasionally Tar Boy had helped himself to another's crab pots or fish trap. Some said he sold dope, but he was never caught. Tar Boy seemed to make money on the edge of legitimacy. With the current price on crabs he did very well. Arthur watched the boat with the black and red buoys piled high head toward shore. He then turned his own boat out through the inlet.

They entered the hook of the cape and circled, watching the depth finder. After anchoring, Arthur said, "Stand here a minute, Rachel, I want to get you good and covered with this suntan lotion." He helped Rachel smear on heavy-duty sunblock and found the girl's hat. He slid off the swim platform, reached up and carried her on his shoulders to shore. The rest of the morning they walked the beach, examining the tide pools and collecting shells.

Back on board, Arthur took her shelling bag and named the shells as she poured them on the boat's aft cabin roof. "Rachel, you know this is a starfish, and these are sand dollars, skate's egg case, witches' pocketbooks, cockle and olive shells."

"Oh Grandpa, look at this big conch. The insides are pink and orange! I want to put this on your sidewalk with your other shells."

"That's a whelk, Rachel. They're often called conchs but that's a common mistake. It'll look fine by the front walk with the others. Did you know all those oyster shells on the walk my daddy or I ate sometime while I was growing up? I think the last whelk to that walk was added when your mamma came to see me in college. Let's change into our swimsuits and go swimming. You can swim, can't you?"

"Uh huh, I mean, yes sir. I took lessons last year. I'll show you." Rachel claimed the aft cabin as her personal dressing room while Arthur used the forward cabin. They swam around in the warm water seeing who could hold their breath the longest. Trying to keep up with her as she became more comfortable with him, Arthur could see child rearing was more than babysitting. Washing off with freshwater on the swim platform at the stern of the boat, they were soon in their shorts and shirts. They ate a late lunch.

31

Arthur pulled a chart from a bag and laid it flat over the aft cabin where they could both see. "This is where we are. Here is Morehead City, Beaufort, Harkers Island, Marshallburg, and right here is our home, Nelson Island. We came through this inlet and we will go back this way." She studied the chart, asking about the numbers and different colors. She identified the channel marks within view.

Rachel explored the rest of the boat as Arthur stowed away the remains of lunch. Arthur started the engine. They circled the cape and entered the waters south of Shackleford Banks. He put the boat on autopilot. "Rachel, let's see if we can catch a fish. For this kind of fishing we don't use bait." He held a plane and spinner and showed her how it worked. "When a fish strikes the hook, the plane will flip up, bringing the weight and the fish to the surface. Here, hold this tight as I drop it out over the side."

She held a device that looked like a wooden 'H' with fish line wrapped through. It served as a hand reel. Rachel unwound the string, watching her grandfather. When the line was almost all out, he tied it to a cleat.

Halfway down Shackleford Banks, Rachel exclaimed, "Grandpa! It's splashing back there." Arthur hauled the line up as Rachel re-wound the line on its wooden reel.

"Guess that'll make a fine meal for us. Do you want to help me clean it?"

"Yuck! No, I'll watch while you do it, Grandpa."

Arthur laughed at the face Rachel made. He tossed the big fish into an ice chest. She glanced behind, fascinated by the wake the boat made when he turned the vessel. The sun streaked the sky with red and orange clouds. She dozed again as he headed toward home.

"Not a bad day," he thought as he looked over at his sleeping grandchild. She clutched the huge shell in her lap. The doll had flipped onto the floor. Already Rachel's cheeks were turning red in spite of the sunblock. He cursed himself, knowing her fair skin shouldn't have been in the sun so long the first time. He was determined not to make the same mistake again.

Later Rachel stood under the shower. "Ahhhh, the water feels like a bazillion needles, Grandpa!" After she dressed in her shorty pajamas he rubbed cool cream on her back, shoulders, and legs. He was relieved to find the sunblock had done its job.

"It's not so bad." She tested her skin by forcing the tender flesh to whiten beneath her finger. It reddened again as she lifted her hand. "It stings a little bit here on my shoulders and cheeks." They sat on the front porch, eating cold shrimp and tuna sandwiches. Without being told, Rachel helped again with the dishes and then climbed the stairs to her room. "Grandpa, I had an awesome day at the beach. Thank you."

"You're welcome, Picklepuss. I had a good time too. Good night." Arthur felt good, like a shaved block of cedar wood. Sharing his private life with someone was a new feeling. He didn't feel restricted having the girl around. He was enjoying his new companion.

Upstairs, Rachel said her prayers, ". . . and thank you for letting me have such a nice grandpa. I don't think I'll be sad anymore. Watch over my parents on their trip. God bless Mamma, Daddy, Grandmother, and Grandpa. Amen."

# Company Coming

During the next several days Arthur kept a close eye on the amount of sun Rachel was exposed to each day. He showed her how to scale and gut a fish and weed his garden. She showed him how to comb her hair in record-breaking time with the least amount of hair pulling. He never seemed to mind the lackadaisical way it fell by midafternoon. She stopped worrying about how it looked.

One morning, while she was making sand paintings on the kitchen table, there was a knock at the screen door. Arthur looked up from his paper. Jesse and Jewel Garner and their big black dog stood at the edge of the porch, their mother a few feet ahead in the shade by the door.

"Arthur Austin, are you going to keep that child to yourself all summer or will you consider letting her get out of your sight for an hour or so? I'm running up to Morehead for some shopping. There's a matinee at the movies. Can we have her for a while?"

Arthur glanced over at his charge and smiled. He had seen that apprehensive smile on her face when she first tried the boiled shrimp. It was a combination of hesitation and optimism. Her eyes were looking down at her artwork but her feet were pulling toward the door.

"Well Rachel, what do you want to do, now that you have options?" Arthur beamed, lifting his bushy white eyebrows. He enjoyed watching her make choices. Jesse and Jewel were standing with their hands and noses on the screen door now. Their grins and laughing eyes were all she needed to make up her mind.

"I'd like to go to the movie, please." Picking up her brushes, Rachel washed them in the kitchen sink. She laid her finished work on the front porch to dry. Then she carefully rolled up the newspapers to keep the sand from spilling.

Jesse picked up one of her finished prints. "Cool, did you do this? It's real pretty."

Rachel grinned at the compliment from the boy. "Sand painting is easy once you get the colors mixed. You add sand to the color and get different stuff depending on how much sand, glue, water and paint you use." Arthur's refrigerator door and walls already displayed her bright artwork.

"I'll tell you what." Arthur got up from his chair and opened the door. "If you can put up with them all, tomorrow we'll invite Jewel and Jesse down for a painting good time." That was a first, him inviting three children to be around all day. He showed Josephine to a chair at the table. The twins sat on the couch while the black dog stood panting on the porch.

"I'll be right back." Rachel raced upstairs.

"We also want to invite her up to visit. We're only two houses up the road. I think we'll enjoy the company. What is she seven, eight years old?" Josephine Garner was a part-time biologist at the Duke Marine Lab in Beaufort. She seemed like a nice girl. Arthur had met her husband at Men of the Church functions.

"How did you all come to live on the island, Josephine? You're from Newport aren't you?"

"Lord, yes, Arthur. We both are but the island offered reasonably priced waterfront property. I work part-time at Duke and Big Jesse works at Cherry Point; well the drive's not bad—we fell in love with the life here. I knew Jesse since we were kids. We wanted children and animals. We never regretted leaving Newport. Island life suits the twins. They have free run of the island with their dog, the cats, pony, and the goat. They share the animal responsibilities and housecleaning chores.

"Sometime I'm going to have to put an anchor on Jesse. He's always going. Jewel stands her own ground, though, if push comes to shove." She smiled over to her two children punching each other on the couch. Her eyes took in the living area and kitchen. "Did you tear a wall out here? I was here when your daddy died. I like what you've done, opening up the view from the kitchen." She stood to walk over to the huge window that looked out over the salty marsh and boat dock. "How deep is it back there? Can you get in and out on low tide?"

"I can only get out during high tide, naturally, but not at the lowest tide." He came across and stood beside her. "Can we still clam over at the old fish factory island or has the state closed that area now?" he said, changing the subject. He and his daddy had dredged out most of the depth behind the house. He was known to back his boat in and out running his big diesel to keep the slip from silting in. Environmentalists frowned on that practice.

"Jesse Sr. and I took the kids over there a few weekends ago. The clamming is great and—say there's another idea. We could all go over there in the skiff and spend an afternoon digging if you want." He was agreeable to the idea. Rachel was going to learn to cook and eat fresh clams, as well as shrimp.

Rachel came down the steps, green plastic purse in hand. She'd changed her clothes to more closely resemble the twins. Arthur reached in his pocket, pulling out a ten-dollar bill.

"No thank you Grandpa, I have my own money," Rachel said.

"Oh, I'm sure you do, but you've been pulling your own weight around here helping me clean house and weed the garden. I reckon this is what I owe you for chores. I was going to pay you something at the end of the month. Let's say this is an advance."

"Thank you Grandpa." Smiling, Rachel slid the bill inside her coin purse. "I guess I'm ready."

The phone rang as the group departed. Arthur walked back into the house and picked up the heavy black receiver. On a premonition, he answered assertively, "Austin here."

"Arthur, dear, how are you? Are you bored with Rachel yet? Do you want me to come take her off your hands? How on earth do you think you're going to manage all summer with a little girl? You know nothing about children. I won't have that child ruined because you don't know any better." He might have agreed with Coral, his former wife, if it had been a week earlier, but now he was enjoying his new role.

He snapped back to the present and answered as stiffly as he could, trying not to let Coral know how much her words bothered him. "We're doing fine here and no thank you about coming down. She's a great kid, Coral. I'm jealous of the fact that you get her the rest of the year," thinking he was giving her a comforting thought to clutch.

"I'll have none of your smooth down east quiet talk, Arthur Austin. Now put the child on and I'll ask her myself if she'd like to come home." He was relieved the girl wasn't there. Before he could respond she went on. "I don't want that child's vocabulary and diction ruined this summer either. I want her to come back to Charlotte without a down east brogue: 'h'oi toid, feesh and sech.' I will not have my granddaughter turned into a little brown sea urchin with islander ways."

She had tried to change him into a "city guy." After the first years of marriage the only things he liked about himself were his coastal roots. He deserted her, his plush job in the family textile plant, and the money it offered, to return to his island. She never told him she was pregnant until the divorce was in progress. He thought it was better for the baby to stay with her mother in Charlotte.

He sent child support, cards and presents over the years that were rarely acknowledged. He received a few pictures of Louise growing up but he was always irritated with her. She became an inconsiderate, spoiled rich kid—like her mother.

In the split second of time that his ex-wife stopped for a breath in her conversation he remembered his first glance of her at Chapel Hill. He remembered her perfume, the feel of her skin, and the softness of her hair. He remembered their weekend trips to the coast, the winter evenings of bonfires on the beach curled in a blanket. He thought she loved him. He found out she had chosen him for his good looks and a college degree from the right university.

She thought her daddy would turn him into whatever it was that fit their family lifestyle. Arthur's own father often said, "If you can't say anything good about someone then don't say anything at all." Arthur had said little about Coral or her family in some thirty years. He wasn't going to let them spoil this child. He was determined to keep this summer and many more his contribution to her growing up.

Coral broke his train of thought. "Arthur, where's Rachel? Put her on now, please." He took a long slow breath and exhaled before he spoke.

"She can't come to the phone right now. She's gone to town with some friends. I'll tell her you called. We've found lots to keep ourselves busy before her parents come back to collect her. Settle down and enjoy your summer. Go to your teas, book clubs, your D.A.R. meetings, and Women's Club activities.

"Let the child enjoy a couple of months at the shore. I'll return her to you none the worse for it. I'm not going to argue with you. Her parents thought she should come to stay the summer, and stay she will. They gave a me an entire package of signed medical forms and fancy parental permission slips that surely cost them an arm and a leg. I have custody of our grandchild for the summer and that's final. I'm going to hang up now and go out to get something for supper. Don't bother calling back. I won't be home."

Arthur replaced the receiver. He went out onto the porch. The telephone began ringing as the screen door slammed behind him.

# Shortcut

It was late afternoon the following day. "I'm really sorry, Arthur. If I'd had any idea this would have happened. Oh, Rachel. My Lord, I didn't think this would happen. She looks okay, don't you think? I'm dreadfully sorry." Josephine Garner was visibly distraught. Rachel stuck her head through the door. Arthur stared at her, stooped down and opened his arms. She ran and clung to him. For the first time he kissed her tear-stained cheeks, enjoying the sweet perfume of a sweaty child. He looked once more at his new Rachel. He suggested she might want to go shower before helping him with supper.

Earlier that day, Josephine had dropped off Jesse and Jewel on her way into Beaufort. The children had immediately spread newspapers on the kitchen table and begun their paintings. Boredom set in by midmorning and the girls decided Arthur needed to redecorate his living room. Jesse shrugged at the idea, but they loaded up the Pink Panther and headed off to Morehead City.

Arthur needed a new cordless hand drill and while he and the boy looked through the shelves of power tools at the new Lowes, the girls dashed off to the curtain and decorating section. He found them reading the dimensions on a package of curtains, comparing them to the slip of paper where they had carefully noted the measurements of his windows. They made another stop at the Super K store and, with a little help from Martha Stewart's summer collections, they purchased sunflower curtains, matching striped throw pillows, an area rug, and quilted slipcovers for the couch and chair. They stopped at Hardee's for burgers and fries. When they came back home an anxious black dog, wagging his tail in the front yard, greeted them. Wobbles didn't bother raising her head until they were out of the truck. Then she slid down from her chair to rub her whiskers on each ankle.

"Let's put them up! Let's hang the curtains." Both the girls were into the project, moving chairs to reach the windows. Arthur plugged in his new purchase, and then went over to help with the old curtain removal. The girls fed the new valances and café curtains through the rods and Jesse re-hung them. They grabbed the worn throw from the couch and daintily unwrapped the new slipcover, spreading it over the couch, tying the arms with straps.

The chair needed to have upholstery tacks and Velcro arm wraps attached. After several tries a chair shape began to emerge as Jesse worked at the girls' direction. The task was finished within the hour. Standing back, they surveyed their handiwork. Smiling, both Rachel and Jewel giggled, "Let's toss this old stuff out into the garbage." Rachel, Jewel and Jesse grabbed up the curtains, worn rug, throw, and wrappings for the trash.

It was approaching four in the afternoon. Knowing Jesse Sr. would soon be home, Rachel asked, "Grandpa, can

I walk home with Jewel and Jesse and help them with their chores? I promise I'll come back as soon as their daddy gets home."

"Yep, Mr. Arthur. Rachel can meet all our animals; we'll even send her home with Dawg. She'll come home when we go in for supper." Arthur judged Jesse might make an effective attorney one day with his argument presentation.

As it was, Jesse Sr. was a bit late. After petting the goat, pony, and assorted menagerie, the children began to feed them. Within seconds the hay started flying. At first a joyful handful of straw was stuck up the back of a shirt. Then a swat of hay came across a face. It was answered in kind. A three-way toss began as hay, hands, children, and barking dog added to the melee.

None of the children could remember exactly when the wad of purple bubble gum went flying out of a mouth. After the shouting and the "fort building" in the hay settled down, Jesse noticed the gum stuck in Rachel's long red hair. The more they tried to separate the hay from the gum, from the hair, the more tangled it became. Jewel ran into the house to get her mother's scissors. When Jesse Sr. pulled into the yard, young Jesse was holding two strands out and Jewel was blithely cutting away. Rachel sat on an upturned milk crate, her mouth cranked sideways in concerned dismay, trying not to flinch as long strands of her red mane landed at her feet.

Josephine arrived within minutes. When Jewel offered the scissors to her she dropped her large satchel and purse. "Go fetch the kitchen stool and sit it right here." Big Jesse lifted Rachel to the stool. She whacked until all the gum and tangles were removed, and then eyed the result. She frowned, and then covered her smiling mouth. Both twins grinned at Rachel.

"Rachel, it doesn't look bad. Why, half the kids going to our school have haircuts worse than yours!" Not realizing Jewel's remark was meant as a compliment, Rachel tried to keep the big tears from sliding down her cheeks.

Jewel ran into the house and came back with a mirror. She held it up while Rachel adjusted the angle. Rachel stared at the face that was watching hers from the reflection. She sat looking at a curly-haired image. The soft red curls sprang from every direction, framing her face. It didn't look as horrible as she had imagined. At least now she wouldn't have to sit each morning to have her hair fixed by her grandfather.

"I think it's just fine. Do you think it'll grow back before my mamma comes to get me? I don't think my grandmother will like it." She paused. "Oh, what will Grandpa say?" She put her hand on her mouth and pulled her eyebrows high into her forehead. "I'd better get home fast."

"Here, hop in my car and I'll drive you back," directed Josephine. As she drove the child the short distance, Josephine became apprehensive. "Let me go in ahead of you to prepare him." She slammed her door and stepped to the porch.

Arthur put his hands in his back pockets and leaned back a little after Rachel had scurried up the stairs. "It doesn't look half bad, Josephine. If you ever lose your job on Piver's Island I guess you can cut hair. I had a devil of a time fixing it in the morning. Some mornings, when she had a rough night of tossing and turning, it'd make a preacher cuss to try to run a comb through that hair. I imagine it'll be a lot cooler, too."

"Oh, Arthur, you are taking this so nicely. The children were only playing. I didn't know how you'd react. I better get on home and help with dinner. The twins have a mess in the barn to rake up. The animals still aren't fed."

He began setting the table. "Why do people think I'm gruff? Haven't I softened in the week since Rachel came?" He was talking to himself when Rachel reappeared.

"Is it really okay, Grandfather?" she asked as she came down the stairs, reverting to her original proper name. He fluffed the top curls already drying in the late afternoon heat. He looked about the newly decorated room and then back to her.

"I like it fine, everything. If you want, I can take you down to the hairdresser's and trim it up some more." She grinned, went to the kitchen drawer, pulled out a dishtowel, tucked it into her shorts and turned around with her hands on her hips.

"What's for supper, Grandpa?"

Arthur smiled back and pulled a large bluefish out of the refrigerator. "Hand me the aluminum foil." Another crisis averted and heaven help him when her mother returned.

# Yard Sale

"Picklepuss, you ever been to a yard sale?" Arthur was reading the paper while Rachel idly flipped the control knob on the television.

They had spent the day driving around the island and over into Beaufort sightseeing. When the bridge to Nelson Island was raised they walked to the edge by the cross arm and waved at the boat passing beneath them. She had never been around so many boats. Some were being built, others repainted.

They had toured one boatyard when Arthur stopped to schedule his annual haul-out for *Lady Lou*. "Rick, when can I bring my boat by for a bottom paint and new zinc?" Arthur asked the lanky young man standing in the huge boathouse door. They scheduled the boat then walked around the yard working their way back to the Pink Panther.

"This place has a lot of different smells, Grandpa." Rachel's nose twitched with the different odors.

"Well, over there is the woodshed. That's where they keep all the timbers to make the framework or keel for a new boat. They make all kinds here: shrimp boats, sportfishing boats, even a paddlewheel. These are made a bit different than the molded ones like my boat. Here they make a wooden boat and then they fiberglass it." She liked the smell of the fresh cut wood in one shed but the bitter fiberglass odor made her eyes water when they peered into the finishing shed. A huge sportfishing boat stood towering above her head, gleaming in the light. Rachel thought about all the new things she was learning about since visiting her grandfather.

"Yard sale, what's that?" Rachel turned the set off and stood by her grandfather as he read.

"Starting at 7:30 A.M., Saturday morning. It's at the elementary school parking lot. We have to go early. I'll bet they'll have something good for breakfast there too."

"What do they sell? I've never been to one before." Rachel wasn't charmed to the idea, yet.

"Everything—clothes, toys, household furniture stuff, boat gear, you name it—and the whole town usually shows up, plus people from the other side of the bridge. Why, this is one of the island's yearly events—sorta like a fair. I bet the Garner twins and Pammy Lee will be there. I know Sarah will have a booth."

"Sounds good to me if Miss Sarah will be there. How early will we have to leave here?" Rachel was an early riser.

The next morning Rachel dressed quickly and came downstairs as Arthur was taking his coffeepot from the stove. "Want some juice or cocoa before we go?"

Rachel went to the refrigerator and took out the plastic juice container. Pouring herself a glass, she took a sip. "Ugh, I just brushed my teeth." She squinched her eyes and pouted her mouth. It was the same face Arthur remembered from his former wife and his daughter many years before.

"Hmmm, well you're ahead of me. Let me pour the rest of this coffee in my thermos mug and brush my teeth. Can you feed Wobbles for me? Check the garden for any new tomatoes. Sit them on the windowsill if they're ready. They'll finish up ripening on the sill." While he shaved, Rachel fed the cat and then strolled out to the garden. When Arthur had finished in the bathroom he found her washing her hands in the kitchen. "Well, it looks like you found a couple out there," he said, nodding at the big green tomatoes.

Although they arrived at the schoolyard at the advertised time, the streets up to the school were already double-parked. Rachel had no idea there were this many people on Nelson Island. Children and adults were milling about the yard. Vendors sat in yard chairs at sawhorse-held plywood tables and card tables. Buyers were picking through piles of clothes and housewares. Arthur saw Belle and her granddaughter exchanging wares at a nearby table. She had an armful of old shirts and a young woman was admiring a shell wreath.

"I want to go over there, Grandpa." Rachel pointed to an area of toys, bicycles, and the Garner twins.

He waved her on with his hand and hollered for her to meet him at Sarah's. Her booth, if not visible by eye, was evident by the long line and smells. She was frying fresh doughnuts in her propane-heated portable deep fryer. As she cooked, one of her assistants poured a white glaze over the already-fried ones. Another helper collected money for the hot pastries and baked goods.

Before he could work his way to the front of the line, Rachel rushed back to him with Jewel in tow. "Morning

Jewel, want a doughnut?" The girl shook her head at Arthur's question.

"Grandpa, can I have a bicycle? I'll pay for it. I'm a good rider. I need to borrow some money from you though, so I can get it now. Miss Jean is holding it for me." Arthur reached the front of the line, nodded to Sarah, ordered two doughnuts and paid. He handed one to Rachel, who had forgotten about her missed breakfast. "Thank you. Come see the bike, ple-ase." She tugged at his hand.

Arthur ambled in the directed path, slowly munching on his hot doughnut. "Rachel, do you have a bike at home? Does your mamma let you ride one?" He didn't want to cross already-established boundaries.

"Mamma doesn't mind me having one. There isn't any-place to ride it where we live so I never got one. I can ride; want to see? There's a helmet that comes with it. Guess what? It's just the right size." Rachel's cheeks flushed with excitement at the idea that she might be the new owner of a two-wheeled vehicle.

"Morning, Jean, what kind of idea have you put into my granddaughter's head this morning?" Arthur brushed the crumbs from his hands and stuffed the sticky napkin in his pocket. "Rachel says you have made her a deal I can't refuse."

"Mr. Arthur," Jesse said as he wheeled up a bright red and silver girl's bike, "I already checked it out. It has five gears. For these sandy back roads it's a good deal. It's almost new, has wide tires. I don't know why someone wants to get rid of it." The boy displayed the bike in the morning light. Arthur rethought the boy's abilities. Perhaps he might make a good salesman.

Arthur crouched his long body down to look over the gears, the tires, and overall sturdiness. Rachel fidgeted, digging her toes into the sand. "Well, how much do you want for this contraption?"

"It's a hundred dollar bike, Arthur, we're asking forty today. Might be more if I have to load it back in my truck and carry it back to the store!" Jean Lewis ran a tight ship at the church consignment shop. She could spot a sucker every time.

"Grandpa, I'll earn the money. Jesse and Jewel and me figure we can wash windows, sell cookies, make deliveries for Miss Sarah, and do other stuff to earn money. Then you don't have to drive me somewhere if I want to go with them down to the bookmobile or the beach." Rachel had her words already worked out. There was little he could do but reach for his wallet. "Here's my ten dollars I didn't spend yet, Grandpa." Rachel held out her money and Arthur added that to the bills he had in his hand.

"Where's the helmet? Here, let's face it out into the playground, away from people, and let me see you ride the thing." He lifted the bike in the opposite direction and Jesse stood beside him as they watched her wobble off in the soft sand.

"Jewel and I will be very careful with her, sir. It's a good bike, better'n mine." Then directing his voice out over the playground Jesse said, "Put'er in a lower gear, Rachel." He ran with his shadow, Jewel, across the yard. Arthur counted his change and put it in his wallet, eyeing the children.

"Well, Jean, guess we've made our major purchase of the day. I want to go look at the boat gear over on the other side. Tell Rachel the direction I'm headed, will ya?" The woman was already busy with another customer, but she nodded her head.

Arthur found a small plow anchor he liked. He was dickering over the price when Rachel found him. Her hair was plastered to her head from the helmet and drops of sweat rolled down her cheek.

"Grandpa, can I ride the bike home? Jesse and Jewel can ride in your truck. I'll go fast and we'll be home in no time." The twins stood back eyeing them both.

"Okay, we'll take the back road that isn't paved yet. There'll be less traffic. You kids tell your mamma where you'll be." They dashed off as Arthur hefted the fifteen-pound anchor up and strolled back to the truck. He looked at his watch. "Not even noon and Lord help me if this turns out to be a not-so-good idea." By the time Arthur and Rachel had reached the truck, the twins had returned with their mother's permission. Arthur pointed out the way and Rachel began the journey towards home.

# Fish Factory Funk

Rachel, Jesse, Jewel, and Pammy Lee were sitting in front of Sarah's store. "I know. Why don't we form a business? Share and share alike." Jesse was having another brainstorm while the girls listened. "We go around the island and ask people what kind of chores they'd like done. You know, like washing windows, weeding gardens, and cleaning out garages and stuff. I bet Miss Sarah and the grocery store have deliveries we can make. We could make a bunch of money now that we all have bikes. We can go everywhere on Nelson Island."

"We did something like that last year but with more of us we could get a lot more jobs," Jewel agreed with her brother.

"Can I do it too?" Pammy Lee was waiting on her grandmother to come out of Sarah's shop. She liked being included in this small group.

"Sure, if I'm going to do it, you can too. Don't we have to ask our parents and, like, my grandpa and your me-maw, Pammy Lee?"

"Yeah, good idea. Let's go home and telephone a few people first to see if we have an interest. Then we already have some customers lined up with jobs. We'll meet back here after lunch, okay?" Jesse assumed the chief executive officer position of the group.

Rachel and Pammy Lee continued to sit on the curb waiting for Belle and Sarah to finish talking. Arthur was meeting Sarah for lunch. They still had a few minutes before he came.

"Belle, are you sure you don't know where your daughter is? She never left anything in writing saying you were to take care of Pammy Lee? There's probably nothing to going to court and requesting guardianship on your own. I don't know anything about it, though. *We'll* have to find out. Have you talked to an attorney?" She paused as she felt a wave of dizziness come over her. "No, they aren't gonna take that youngun away from you. Stop your fretting."

Sarah was trying to relieve Belle's mind but at the same time she was agitating her own. "My goodness, I feel out of breath thinking about all this." She patted her chest and stopped talking to take a few deep breaths. Sarah put her hands to her cheeks, feeling them flush.

"Sarah, are you alright? Brandy, bring Miss Sarah a glass of water please." Belle pushed her friend down into a chair and was wringing a damp towel out for her face when Arthur and the children came in the door. "Here, put this on your forehead. You've got all upset worrying about my problems." Belle turned to a speechless Arthur. "Do you think we ought to get her to the hospital?"

"Nonsense, hush now. I got a bit excited. Let me sit here and rest a bit. Brandy, honey, can you take over for me for a while?" During the summer months Sarah had hired a new woman to work part-time. Brandy quietly nodded and stood back watching. "Now, Arthur, you and Rachel are taking me to lunch like you promised. Belle, call a lawyer about what we talked about. We'll talk later." Sarah stood, slowly testing her balance, and reached for Arthur's arm. "Let's walk out to your truck and don't give me no sass."

Concerned, Arthur walked Sarah out and lowered her into the passenger side. Rachel went around to the driver's side and slid in before Arthur. "Drive us to the diner, hon," Sarah said as he put the keys in the ignition. "I think I'd like a cool glass of lemonade."

Seated in a booth, they reached for menus. "Funny, I must need glasses. I can hardly read the print here. Rachel, can you read the special of the day off this sheet for me?"

"Sarah, I don't like the sound of what I'm hearing. Your face is still flushed. Now you're telling me you have blurred vision. How long has this been going on?" Arthur said, expressing his concern.

"Oh, I'm sure it's nothing. I got overheated and I'm getting this splitting headache right now. I guess my eyes don't want to adjust. Maybe all I want is some crackers with my lemonade. Rachel, what do you want for lunch? Arthur, really, let me sit for a while. Order our lunch while I relax. You both stop staring at me now. Let's please get back to normal." She sighed and sat back in her seat as they ordered. The food came; Sarah nibbled on a plate of chicken salad and sipped at her drink. When they had finished, Arthur drove Sarah back to her shop. He parked and helped her up the back stairs to her apartment.

"Sarah, you lie down now. Rachel, watch while I go down and explain to Miss Brandy that Miss Sarah is going to be up here the rest of the day."

"No Arthur, I want to rest a few minutes. I'll go back to work in a bit," Sarah objected.

"Like hell you are. If you get out of that bed it's to go to the doctor's. Now lie down and relax. Rachel, you holler for me if she tries to get up." He took one last look at her before he left. Rachel positioned herself in the lounge chair by the door and stood guard until he returned.

While downstairs, Arthur called her doctor in Beaufort. He described Sarah's symptoms over the phone and scheduled an appointment for her later in the week. When he returned Sarah was asleep. He motioned Rachel to follow him down the steps.

"Grandpa, is Miss Sarah going to be alright?" Rachel whispered.

When they reached the bottom of the stairs, the twins and Pammy Lee met them. "Mr. Arthur, how is Miss Sarah?"

"I don't know, son. We'll find out when she goes to the doctor." His face showed concern, so Jesse wisely chose to leave the new business venture until another day. "You kids go on and play now. Rachel, I'll be home about five this evening. Pammy Lee, tell your me-maw I'll call her later." Arthur returned up the steps and slipped quietly into the apartment.

"Well, we could go to my house. There's always stuff to do, if you wanna?" Pammy Lee offered.

"Wow, really? I've always wanted to go inside your house. It looks so cool." Jesse grabbed up his bike. Each child stood still long enough to put on his or her helmet before riding to the eastern end of Nelson Island. They yodeled, sang and laughed their way along the road as they approached the Nelson mailbox. It was a carved loon, its hind end dropped down for the door. If mail needed to be picked up, a wing was raised into position. Huge abandoned pilings, gray driftwood and more wood sculptures filled the yard. They felt like they were entering a museum. Jesse,

Jewel, and Rachel began to whisper as they approached the front door.

"Awesome." Jewel ducked under a wind chime made from scrap PVC pipe and tin. Other wind chimes and mobiles drifted in the breeze as they walked by. The heavy metal door slid open as they approached. Belle recognized the visitors as friendly.

"Hi, Pammy Lee, Rachel, Jesse, Jewel. Y'all come on inside. Now tell me what you're up to. If you don't have anything planned for the afternoon I was making some sand castings. You can watch. Maybe you want to try your hands in it too?" As the children filled her in on their business plans and Sarah's status, Belle pulled trays, buckets of sand, and paints from a large closet.

She mixed a soup-like plaster in a bucket and showed them how she used shells, sticks and imagination to design her wall sculptures. As the children watched she pressed images into the sand trays. The phone rang and Pammy Lee took over the responsibility of showing them how to continue. She had often helped her grandmother make shell candleholders, wall plaques and sea witch faces. The four children tried making their own after watching the process a few times and studying the results. Their art pieces were combination face-shell images.

Belle returned. "Why, you kids learn fast. These will be fine when we turn them out. Help me pour the plaster in— gently now or you'll mess up your imprints. If you mess them up don't worry. We'll do a bit of plastic surgery later on. While they harden, would you like a tour of our home?" Neither Belle nor Pammy Lee could remember when they last entertained company or showed off their home. They climbed stairs up to the topside, where they viewed the entire end of the island and the sound beyond. They went

from room to room, amazed by the sunlit rooms with bold-
ly painted wall murals.

"Wow, this is awesome! You should charge admission
to see this place. It's unbelievable. Pammy Lee, you sure
are lucky to have a grandma like Miss Belle." Jesse was fascinated with every aspect of the converted fish factory.

"I like your room best, Pammy Lee." Jewel lingered a
bit, admiring the suspended bed and turret with windows.
Painted like a castle, the decorated walls showed storybook
fairy princesses.

"I started it for my children, and now my grandchildren
enjoy it. You promise me one thing. Don't you tell anyone
else but your parents about what we have here. I don't have
time for guided tours. You hear?" Belle returned to her
semi-grumpy tone of voice as she and her grandchild
escorted them to the door. "Now come back in two days
after lunch and we'll finish up these projects, okay?"

Rachel couldn't wait to get home to tell Arthur about
her afternoon. He half-listened to her stories of the wonderful fish factory-turned-home. When the phone rang after
dinner, he was relieved to hear Sarah was resting well. He
kissed Rachel good night and went to sit on the porch. He
thought what his life would be like without Sarah or
Rachel. He wasn't too pleased with the resulting picture.
Yawning, he rose, went inside, and closed the door against
the night and his thoughts.

# Island Do-Bees

"Sarah's going to the doctor for tests, Rachel. I want to be there. Do you have enough to do today?" Arthur had already dressed and eaten when Rachel came down the steps. "I've made you a sandwich to take when you go off. Miss Josephine said she'd look after you until I get back. Honey, do you mind that I'll be gone all day?"

Rachel was already drinking her juice as Arthur talked. She shook her head, "Nope, I mean, no sir. We have a long list of things to do today—washing cars and making deliveries. We keep in touch with walkie-talkies. Two of us are always together. Don't worry about me.

"We have enough work to do. We'll be busy the rest of the summer. We printed flyers on the Garner's home computer and passed them out on the street or stuck them in doors. For large jobs like washing a house's windows, we all do it."

Arthur dropped Rachel off, and then drove to Sarah's. They took her van to Beaufort. "Arthur, thanks for bringing me. I feel fine today. Well, a bit tired. See, no blurred vision and no headaches. You shouldn't worry about me. Isn't that a switch? I'm the 'token worrier' for everyone else."

"Hush up, woman, and allow me to indulge you in some concerned pampering." Arthur held her hand in the waiting room and tried to clear his mind of troublesome thoughts. They were sent from the doctor's office to the hospital and back again to the doctor's where they waited again. After a final talk with the doctor they were allowed to leave. Stress seemed to be the key culprit. A new diet, without caffeine, lowered salt intake and stress reduction were prescribed.

"I've been wired, pricked, jabbed, stabbed, photographed, and listened to. I've played all their silly stand-on-one-foot, touch-my-nose games. What an ordeal! How does lunch sound? I haven't eaten since last night. Arthur, take me somewhere dark and romantic for lunch." Sarah was glad to be through.

"I know just the spot." He pulled into a local drive-in and placed an order; after that he drove to a waterfront park. They enjoyed the lunchtime view of boaters at the launch ramp. It wasn't romance he wanted at that moment, merely a diversion from the morning's activities.

"The doctor said I have to get my blood pressure down. I don't think these French fries are what I need," Sarah giggled as she bit into the burger. "I'll start tomorrow. He also said to cut back on caffeine. I never thought about how much coffee and iced tea I drink. I know I should be concerned, but I have too many other things to worry about now. I . . ."

"Sarah, I've never said much about the way you run your life, but you need to slow down. I sat there with you and listened to that doctor. You heard what you wanted. You take on too much and I'm here to tell you that I care enough about you to interfere in your business now, if I think it's justified." Arthur was surprised at his own words.

Sarah pursed her lips, sitting quietly. She rolled the greasy sandwich wrapper up and stuffed it into the paper sack from which it came. As she brushed a few crumbs from her skirt, she could feel the heat rising in her face. Arthur Austin had no right to tell her what to do. However, the longer she sat she realized he was right. She hated to admit it. Her mind was already back at the island deciding how she could rearrange her work and cut back on her responsibilities to relax a bit. This new attitude Arthur assumed was unsettling.

Maybe she should rethink their relationship. "I appreciate your concern Arthur, but I don't like being pushed by someone else. I've been a widow over ten years. I'm not used to answering to anyone, not even you." Arthur finished his lunch then drove back to the island. It was a quiet forty-minute drive. He deposited Sarah at her door without another word.

# Snake in the Crabpot

Tar Boy Willis was hopping mad. It took over four hours to find all his buoys. After that, he circled back, picking up his exposed crab pots on Middle Marsh. "There weren't no call to do what they done and someone's gonna pay." He talked to himself as he approached his home. Sure he had helped himself a time or two to the crabs of another man's pot, but times were slim.

"A man's gotta do what a man's gotta do. Damn!" he hissed to himself as he hit his damaged hand on the boat wheel. He cut himself tugging in the last few crab pots. He wrapped his hand in a kerosene-soaked rag to stop the bleeding. "There's no call for that kind of meanness and besides to leave the one buoy still attached to the last crab pot." When he pulled it up there was a big copperhead coiled in the bait well, dead, but the message was clear.

There was one place on the island where every waterman ended his working day. It was now late afternoon. He figured that whoever was responsible would have an eye on the river to see him return—to see what his reaction would be.

"Yes, you boys stand there in the shadows of that fish house. Oi'm a coming." They were stacking their boxes and buckets, emptied from their catches. Some were still wearing their long waders over grubby tee shirts. Most hadn't shaved; crabbers started early in the morning. A few were smoking along the back dock. He saw a finger point his way. A chuckle rose across the water to meet him.

"Alright. Which one of you sons of bitches did it? Come clean! Oi'll take you on now, right here." He threw a line over a piling and pulled himself up, throwing the straps of his own waders off his shoulders, and shucking his boots on the edge of the dock. His filthy toes felt the sun-warm deck.

"What's got into you, Tar Boy? You look moighty mad for some reason." One of the Davis brothers nudged the other and grinned. "Want some help with that there load of crabs yew brought in? Lemme give yew some help." He reached out an open hand. Tar Boy struck it away. Davis feigned a look of surprise and shook his head.

"What the hell yew done that fer? I'se offering to help yew with your load. What yew got there in that big basket of yours, Tar Boy? Hey, fellers, looks like Tar Boy has a new trade. Looks like he's been a'snaking. Not even a feesh or a crab in the basket. Is that it Tar Boy? Yew quit the crabs and took up snake hunting? What they getting for snakes these days?"

Tar Boy took another swipe at the man and missed. "I'll show you what for. Any man who messes with my crab pots'll find hisself with a live snake in his boot if he wants to play rough. Oi know where you dock." His lazy eye roved from one face to another. The other men, not saying a word, stood up and circled the distraught man. Tar Boy took a step backwards. "You hadda do it didn't you? You go out there.

You cut all the floats off my pots and then you put that bugger in the last one." He realized he was only one against a gang of unhappy fishermen. His words flung faster now than his fists.

"Mike Taylor here says he saw you pulling in someone else's pots the other day, Tar Boy. Kelso Smith has come up more often short on his haul too. Their pots are over where you put yours down. In fact, a bunch of us here are coming up short these days and wonder if it's some sticky-fingered tar boy been out there to those pots claiming the crabs as his own. Billy says you always come in loaded up with crabs. At the price they're bringing, that's more than a crime, Tar Boy. You're stealing a man's pride in feedin' his family and paying his bills. I don't know about the rest of these boys here, Tar Boy. If you're seen doing it again I'm here to tell you it'll be the last pot you pull, I guaran-damn-tee you that." One of the Davis brothers took a step toward the smaller man.

Tar Boy eyed the distance between himself and his boat and backed toward it carefully. "You threatening me, Davis? Here in front of all these witnesses? Are you saying a few crabs is all you're upset about? Boys, boys, now let's not get all worked up. Oi come up short a few days moiself. Overfishing they say. Pollution. Why them crabs ain't out there like they used to be."

He eased himself back into his skiff, pulling his waders down beside him. "Oi can see you're all worked up on the matter. Someone's fed you a pack of lies. Oi got me a mess of work to do this evening, fixin' all these pots. Oi best be getting to it. Oi'm sure the crabs are out there, fellers. You have to be patient. Find spots no one goes. That's what Oi do. Don't be pickin' on me cause Oi get lucky a few days." He pushed the start button on his console. With an eye to the fish house, he backed his boat into deeper water. Tar

Boy pushed the throttle forward. His boat surged in the water, leaving a wake that bounced the other fishing skiffs off the fish house dock.

# Break

"Now you kids be good." Josephine was home for the day. Rachel had spent the night at the Garner's. After breakfast she called her grandfather to extend her stay, passing a rainy morning with the twins. The woman grabbed her purse on her way out the door. "I won't be gone long. I'm running to the grocery store. I'll be right back."

The children played quietly only a few minutes before Jesse laughed. "Ha, Jewel, give me all your money. Welcome to Hotel City. Gotcha good!" He continued to goad his sister.

"I don't like playing Monopoly with you Jesse, you play too mean." Jewel threw down her little silver dog piece and ran upstairs. Rachel slid from her chair as Jesse shrugged and began to gather the money and assorted pieces into the box.

"Hey, Rachel, want to play Clue?" asked Jesse. Rachel shook her head then followed Jewel up the stairs to her room.

"You okay, Jewel? He plays different than my mamma or grandmother ever played. I think it's something about being a boy." She sat on her friend's bed and waited for some response.

After a while Jewel shrugged, "Oooh, I'm okay." Hearing her brother outside her door, she said, "Sorry Jesse. I don't like losing so much."

"What else you want to do?" Jesse stuck his head into the room. "Mamma asked me to clean the mess out of the attic this week. Let's surprise her before she gets back. Three can finish a lot faster than one. Come on." He led the way.

Piled in the attic were old cardboard boxes, newspapers, faded wrapping paper and discarded toys. By now the rain had stopped. The attic steamed from the morning heat and dampness. After making two trips down and out, Jesse had an idea. "Hey, I'll throw it down the steps to you, Rachel. You throw it down to Jewel. We can get it downstairs and then carry it all outside. It'll be a lot less work and climbing in this weather." The disappearing staircase soon became a garbage chute. Rachel stood below trying to catch or stop things before they marked a wall or broke.

"That should do it." Jesse came down the fold-down steps carrying an old football helmet. "Now, I've got a better idea. Have you ever been to Waterworld, Rachel? They have these slides where you sit on an old sack and ride down. I bet these old boxes will make good sliders. Let's try it."

"Jesse, what are you doing?" Jewel called from the hallway, looking up at her brother at the top of the steps, standing in a box with a helmet on his head. "No, Jesse, you better not. Mamma will really be mad if you break anything!" She rushed up the steps to grab her brother's shirt as he squatted inside the box.

"Chicken, Jewel. Are you gonna be a scaredy cat? Ain't nothing gonna get broke. There ain't nothing at the bottom of these stairs but that wall down there. That'll stop us from going further. Watch, I'll go first." Without hesitating, he leaned back in the box and shimmied down the carpeted stairs. "Whee, what a ride! Wanna go next, Rachel?"

Rachel stood at the top now looking down at her friend. Still skeptical, she asked, "Did it hurt when you went down?"

He climbed back up the stairs and selected another box. "Naw, you sit back in the corner and lean on your butt. Here, you put this on your head. You'll be fine." He snapped the strap beneath her chin as she climbed into the next box.

"No, Rachel, Jesse, someone's gonna get hurt." Jewel looked skyward and said a prayer. Rachel was launched.

Thump. Thump. Thump. Rachel landed on her head, denting a four-inch hole in the wall. She flipped out of the box. "AWAH! Oh no. I made a hole in your Mamma's wall. Uh-oh, I can't move my hand, Jesse." Her left arm lay at her side.

"Don't move, Rachel, Jewel, run go get Mr. Arthur. Don't move Rachel, oh my God. I'm calling 911." Frantically Jesse jumped over the box and the girl on the floor, and ran to the phone.

Josephine and Arthur arrived a few minutes behind the local rescue squad. Arthur had just started weeding in the garden when Jewel came running and hollering into the yard. Josephine saw the ambulance go by the grocery parking lot as she was putting her bags in the car.

"It's alright, Mrs. Garner, Mr. Austin. This is one tough little girl. If I'm not mistaken she has a clean break in her upper arm, but x-rays will tell. We don't want her jolting and pushing that broke bone through her skin. She gets to ride in the ambulance to Morehead City. Mr. Austin, you want to ride with us?" The EMT made a note on a clipboard then transmitted a message on her radio to the hospital.

"Yes, of course." Arthur could see his white-faced granddaughter being carried from the house.

"Grandpa, it doesn't hurt. I punched a hole in Miss Josephine's wall. I'm sorry." She still wore the football helmet.

Arthur was confused. "How'd this happen?" He looked at the twins who stood in the drive.

Josephine took each child's hand and said, "Arthur, we'll follow behind the ambulance. This is a story we both want to hear."

At the hospital, Rachel was taken to be x-rayed. Arthur sat at the registration desk answering questions. Luckily, he grabbed the packet of legal papers before leaving his house. The clerk helped him find medical cards and insurance information. Afterward he came towards the Garners and sat in a cold plastic chair.

"It's my fault, Mr. Arthur, I told her to do it. Mamma, I'm sorry about the wall. I'll pay for it. I wasn't thinking. I'm really sorry, Mamma. What did they say about Rachel? Will she be alright?" Visibly distraught, the pale-faced boy sank in his chair.

Arthur, finally thinking of the boy and not Rachel, thought he saw the humility of a new preacher in his face. "Hmm, Jesse how about you telling me everything that happened? If he leaves anything out, Jewel, you fill me in." He sat in a chair across from the youth, looking Jesse right in the eye as he began the story.

After both twins were finished, Arthur couldn't help but smile thinking of the children sliding down the steps in the box, wearing a football helmet for protection. "Is that so?

Well I reckon your mamma and daddy will have to deal with you, son. Josephine, excuse me, I see the lady up there motioning for me."

"Mr. Austin, the doctor says you can come back now." The brightly-bloused woman looked over her glasses, giving him a reassuring smile. She led him into one of the many small rooms. An x-ray hung on a lighted panel. Rachel, without the football helmet, was on the examining table.

"Hello, Picklepuss, how you doing?" Arthur bent to kiss her, brushing a tear from her cheek. He turned to the doctor, "I'm the girl's grandfather, Arthur Austin." He shook the doctor's hand.

"Ah, so you're this half-pint quarterback's guardian. She's been telling me quite a story about her summer so far. That picture tells the rest of the story." He pointed to the x-ray. "She's very lucky. We're going to put a pretty cast on her arm. She needs to keep it out of the water. No showers for a while. I'll have the nurse make up an instruction sheet for you to follow. She's going to be as good as new." To Rachel he said, "Young lady, no more riding down stairs in boxes and no more football, got that?"

"Yes, sir. Grandpa . . ." she began.

"Shush, be still. There's nothing for you to worry about." Arthur held her hand as they began to work on the cast.

Later that evening Arthur called Coral first, then Sarah with the report. "Sarah, I have a request. I need you to move in here for a few days until we get straight. Don't interrupt me now; I need you more than I ever thought I did. I have a story you're not going to believe."

# Pony Penning

The July day was barely beginning. Already the gnats and mosquitoes not driven off by the night breeze were hugging the screen door. The curtains, which usually flapped in the southwest breeze, hung limp at the window edge. Six green tomatoes, pulled from a vine, sat on the sill. When they turned red, Arthur and Rachel would slice them onto heavily-mayonnaised bread. The smell of coffee brewing sneaked through the house. The black skillet sat waiting on the stovetop.

Arthur was at the table reading the day's paper, squinting at the poorly lit print. He forgot to turn on the overhead light before settling down with his first cup of coffee. The days were already getting shorter. His bare feet tapped the linoleum floor. The gray cat rubbed her side up against the screen door, causing it to slap impatiently against the sill.

Outside a car door slammed. Arthur shifted in his chair to peer into the front yard. "That you, Smitty?" He reached for another ceramic mug hanging in the enamel-painted cabinet. Opening the refrigerator he brought out a can of evaporated milk, placing a clean spoon on the drain board. His friend opened the door; mindful of the cat trying to sneak in, he pushed her aside with his toe.

"Lord 'a mercy, but it's gonna be a hot one today, Arthur. Are ya sure you want to go down East this morning?" Smitty put two heaping spoons of sugar in his cup. He added milk until he emptied the can, and then poured in the coffee. His friend brewed a strong cup of coffee. Besides, Smitty liked it sweet.

Arthur heard the commode flush upstairs. His friend, if not the morning sun, woke his granddaughter. Rachel would be dressed and down soon. He moved to the egg basket to grab a handful of eggs.

"Have you eaten yet?" Arthur asked.

"Margaret fed me a tiny bran muffin this morning and already I feel a big space down there. Don't mind if I join you and the little one, Arthur; thanks for asking. I should return the favor for you. I eat here often enough." Smitty reached into the dish rack, found another place setting, and folded a paper towel for his napkin at his usual chair.

"Well looky here! Looks like something the cat drug in." He reached out to grab the girl's hair. Smiling sheepishly, she quickly dodged his hand. She held her hairbrush in one hand. She was having trouble snapping one of the grippers on her denim shorts. Her grandfather reached down and snapped the strap in place, then took the brush and smoothed down the fine red hair. He'd make sure she wore her baseball cap today to keep the sun off her face.

Wearing a cast, Rachel could now dress and get around as before. Sarah had stayed over a week, helping her dress and bathe as needed. She needed help with zippers and buttons but was able to dress herself. Arthur fashioned plastic bags that kept her cast from getting wet in the shower and at the beach.

After a two-week grounding and lecture of undetermined consequence, Jesse and Jewel were allowed to visit. By this time Rachel had learned to balance her cast on the top of her head, keeping it out of the water when she was at the beach. She could even ride her bicycle without toppling over. She was the only child on the island whose underarm was as brown as the rest of her. She returned to the doctor's once for a checkup. The cast was replaced because it got too wet. When they cut it off, sand and a few small shells fell out, which she saved in her small jewelry box.

"What's for breakfast, Grandpa?" She eyed the smoking grease already floating in the pan and the stack of slightly burnt but very crisp bacon on the paper towel beside it. He was whisking up a mess of scrambled eggs in a clear glass bowl. Earlier he laid out bread on a cookie sheet. She jammed a dishtowel in her shorts front and proceeded to butter the bread and then stick it into the oven as he turned the frothy mix into his hot skillet.

Rachel smiled to herself. The first time she'd seen him cook eggs in hot bacon grease she had turned up her nose. Now she was used to the salty bacon-flavored eggs. It was a part of staying here that she enjoyed—cooking breakfast with her grandfather. As she watched through the glass window in the oven door the bread began to brown quickly. She expertly removed the pan with an oven mitt and stacked the toast on a small plate. The eggs hardened and Arthur spooned them into the individual plates. "When are we going to see the ponies?" She stuffed a bite of eggs in her mouth as soon as he finished saying grace.

"Well, them boys have been up there with their horses and boats since before light. If we get there too early, they won't be across the sound yet. It'll get pretty hot standing there waiting for them to come in."

Besides fireworks, every Fourth of July the locals sponsored a pony penning, rounding up the remaining herds on the nearby islands. The banker ponies were driven across the sound between a channel lined with local boaters. When they reached shore, the ponies were urged into the long gaping aluminum gates of a temporary corral, where they were singled out for the sale. They were checked for sickness and given medical attention if needed. The non-selling healthy stock were let loose after the auction.

He wanted to avoid taking her early because sometimes a horse was injured during the event. Frequently a horse had to be destroyed due to illness or a bad wound created by the confusion of such a large herd in one fenced area. He knew the hour-long trip would be too short a delay and tried to think up an excuse for a later start. Reading his friend's mind, Smitty piped up.

"Rachel, would you like to go see the soft-shell crabs they raise up at the point? We can go see the ponies after that. I might be persuaded to buy you a Popsicle after we see those crabs."

The girl's mouth stayed to the side of her face. She knew the sooner she could get the two men out of the house and on the way, the closer she was to seeing ponies. Maybe she would get to ride one. She sopped up the remaining strawberry jam with her last piece of toast and nodded yes, her red curls flopping up and down. "I guess so. Can we leave now, Grandpa?" Her leg stuck to the plastic seat as she slid to the floor.

"Hold your horses. We got dishes to wash and you haven't brushed your teeth. Did you make up your bed?"

"Yep." She danced her plate to the sink and ran back to place the butter and jam in the refrigerator. She grabbed the

dishcloth on the sink before the older man could comman-
deer it for dish duty. She wiped the table, chairs and counter
around the stove.

He rinsed the glasses and ran the dishwater, watching
her with a keen eye. "Don't brush those crumbs on the floor.
They'll make a mess."

"I've already figured that out," she said as she ran to the
door and let in Wobbles and Dawg, both heading for the
table crumbs. She grinned as she watched their licking, tap-
ping her foot at a bit of toast they missed. "Now, out you
both go." She scrammed them both from the kitchen before
the men could hide their grins. "I'll clean up the living
room. Then I'll brush my teeth."

Her grandfather shook his head, removing a mop from
the utility closet and holding it beneath the hot running
water. "Don't forget to bring down your hat and your suntan lotion when you come," he reminded her.

"You have to admit, Arthur, she got that one past you,"
Smitty chuckled, watching his friend wipe up tongue and
toe prints from the four legged crumb-busters. The grandfather finished the dishes and wiped his hands on the towel
stuck in the front of his britches. He tucked the towel into
the range door handle and finished his last gulp of coffee.
He ran his hand over his chin, deciding to forego the morning shave. He looked around to make certain the house was
in good order.

His friend watched him dump the coffee grounds into
the metal trashcan, its lid held up by some foot-pressure
contraption. The lid clamped down on the plastic bag hanging over the edge. "You sure know how to handle that little
squirt, I have to say that. When you told me she was coming to stay the summer with you, I didn't think you'd make
it through the first week."

Before Arthur had a chance to respond, Rachel bounced down the last steps, "I'm ready!" He checked to make certain the stove was off, grabbed up her backpack, and gestured Smitty through the door, not bothering to lock it on the way out.

✿ ✿ ✿

Mrs. Brown and her husband were old friends of Arthur. "Lord 'a mercy would ya look at that youngun's red hair." Rachel liked to hear them talking with their down east brogue. It took a while for her ears to adjust to their conversation. "I b'lieve she takes after you, Arthur. Does she have the temperament to go with that red hair?" He ignored her comment and thanked her for the blackberry pie she had sent on her husband's last visit.

Never one to accept a compliment, Mrs. Brown spread her hands on her canvas apron and promised him a mess of bluefish next time. "Be careful, honey, watch your fingers," she said to Rachel. Then to Arthur and Smitty she asked, "Why you reckon children like to touch 'em? They always got to put their hands in the water." She shook her head as she nudged a pile of crabs with a gloved hand. The crabs scuttled to the other end of the trough or piled on one another.

The water pumped over the crabs twenty-four hours a day, leaving the Browns with long workdays. They were up most of the night and early in the morning tending to both the crab pots and the bins. The crab growing arenas appeared to be several tiered bunk beds, water constantly running throughout. At the point of shedding their shells the crabs were marked, graded, and moved out. "Well, Rachel honey, I b'lieve you've seen the whole show. Do you have any questions? If I don't know the answer, I'll get Harlan out here. He's my boy. He thought up this whole mess and it seems to be doing what he claimed."

They waved good-bye to the woman and headed off in Smitty's car. "The crab factory outing was a good idea, Mr. Smitty."

They stopped at the Island Store for their Popsicle and sat on a bench, in the shade of a nearby tree, sucking on the cold pops. Rachel sucked on an orange one that made an orange line around her mouth with a few drips down her front. Arthur and Smitty split a grape one, Smitty splurging on the purchase. "I thought you'd like it. You climbed up into near about every bin they had, watching that water flow between them."

After wetting their hands under a nearby artesian well, they wiped their hands on their pants. They drove off with her sitting between them. As they reached the end of the island, they noticed a line of parked cars.

Some people were carrying grease-soaked paper plates with fried fish, hushpuppies and coleslaw. The meal was the second reason people came from as far away as Greensboro, Raleigh, and beyond.

Politicians in short sleeves with loosened ties pumped hands and slapped backs. Sweat streamed down their hat-less heads. The food was plentiful and the occasion was exciting. Lanky cowboys straddled lean banker horses, riding through the crowd. The noise, dust, and commotion were enough to cause one to stay in the cool air-conditioned car, but Rachel was out the door running toward the pen with no hesitation.

By now the older mares and stallions had been separated from the selling stock. Someone brought in several buckets of water for the remaining ponies. The bravest ventured over and sucked up the cool wetness. The rest stood their ground, some shaking in fright at the noisy crowd of people leaning over the fence gawking at them or bidding on the last animals. The noise and dusty horses disappointed Rachel. Dust and flies filled the air and clung to her face. Sweat droplets ran through her hair and down her face as she peeked through the fence rails. The cast on her arm felt heavier in the heat. She wearied of the sight and backed out to find her grandfather talking with a man on a horse. She sidled over to him, rubbed her forehead on his shirt and struck her quiet sulking pose. He put his hand on her shoulder. She wasn't listening to the conversation. She could hear the down east accent and a few words, but she was paying more attention to the stream of sweat running down the big horse's chest and legs. He stamped his foot and swished his tail to rid himself of annoying flies. She could smell the heat of the horse and the leather of the saddle.

Surprised, Rachel hollered when her grandfather lifted her up and sat her in front of the rider. She had never been so high. She had ridden ponies but never a horse! She wiped the horse's neck with now-dirty hands. The wrangler walked the horse out of the crowd, down the road towards the long eating tables that had been set up under tents. Arthur and Smitty followed at a safe distance.

"Well, Arthur, you could always make room for a stall in that garage of yours." Smitty grinned at his friend.

Arthur shook his head and reached in his back pocket for his wallet. "Lemme buy you lunch today, Smitty. You drove us here."

His friend patted his stomach and smiled in anticipation as he watched the little redheaded girl, cap askew, holding a handful of mane and grinning as she rode toward the food tent. "Never one to say no, Arthur."

# Au Pair

"Mom says we need an au pair so we don't get into any more trouble." Jesse dug his worn open-toed sneaker into the dirt of the garden. A young woman came up the path toward Arthur's house with Jewel. Rachel and Arthur looked up. She looked no more than sixteen to Arthur. She had long brown hair clipped up into a knot on the back of her head. Her nose was covered with white cream, but freckles peeked through, across her cheeks. She wore a thin-strapped knit shirt over flowered beltless Bermuda shorts. "She's nothing more than a glorified babysitter if you ask me," Jesse shrugged.

"Hi, I'm Meredith Wade. I'll be staying with the Garners until the end of the semester in August." She put her hands on her hips, exasperated at the boy's remark.

Jesse squatted down and pulled a weed from the base of a tomato plant. Today he wore his swim trunks as shorts. His sister wore shorts over her bathing suit, Velcro-strapped sandals and a wide brim soft hat.

Arthur lifted himself carefully from his bent position, wiped his hands on the back on his pants and offered his hand. "I'm Arthur Austin and I guess you know Rachel."

"I'm watching over the twins for a while. I get a place to stay free. I'm at the Duke lab this summer while I'm doing research on horseshoe crabs. Today, I need some help. Would it be okay with you if Rachel went with us over to Carrot Island to count crabs? The twins said she might like to come. I'm good with a boat. I've already packed us a lunch."

Rachel looked at Jewel. "I promised I'd help Grandpa in the garden and later we were going to finish the pickles we're making." Her hat was askew over her red curls. Rachel looked at her grandpa. She hated to disappoint Jewel but at the same time felt obligated to help her grandfather.

Jewel reached over and touched Rachel's hand. "Don't you wanna come?"

Arthur patted Rachel's shoulder. "I can wait to do the pickles tonight when you come home if you want to help." To the young woman he said, "We were going to jar and make up the syrup to finish off the fourteen-day pickles."

Wobbles came out for an ankle rub all around. Rachel reached down, running the cat's tail between her fingers absentmindedly. She lifted a sandaled foot and scratched her ankle. She looked at Jewel and then at her grandfather.

"I guess I can go if you promise to wait for me before you do the pickles. I really want to have a jar of pickles I made to take home to show Grandmother and my mom and dad. They *never* let me make pickles." She was learning a lot of new things since coming to the island.

She had new play clothes, a new haircut, new friends, and a cat that liked her. She had new responsibilities. She had decorated Grandpa's living room. She had learned to bait a hook, clam, and grow flowers in the garden. Now she was helping to make pickles and count horseshoe crabs!

"Wait until I change into my bathing suit and get my things. Jewel, want to come with me?" She grabbed the older girl's hand and they dashed up the porch steps.

"We can go inside where it's cooler or would you like to sit on the porch? I've got a pitcher of sweet tea in the refrigerator. Would you like some?" While they waited on the girls, Meredith explained about the enzyme in horseshoe crabs that acted as an anticoagulant and some of the other uses they were discovering.

"Years ago, I found hundreds along every sound and island shore but recently they're being harvested at an alarming rate to be used as bait and for laboratory tests. The lab has received a grant to evaluate their future numbers and habits," Meredith continued. For the first time, Jesse saw an advantage in his new guardian. Maybe she wasn't such a problem after all. This could be interesting and fun.

After the three left, Arthur returned to his garden. He took his glass of tea to finish while he worked. Wobbles was already asleep in the shade. A slight breeze blew from the east. The sky showed clumps of puffy clouds. "Buttermilk sky," Arthur muttered, noting the wind's change of direction. "It'll probably rain within twenty-four hours, Wobbles." He finished his work in the garden, cleaned up, changed clothes, and rode into town. At the Taylor Fish House, Billy brought him up to date on the problem with Tar Boy.

Arthur stopped to check on Sarah and found her working on a dripping spigot. While he fixed it, she made him a turkey sandwich and root beer. Arthur liked their unspoken arrangement. "You know what Rachel asked me when she first met you? Well I never thought, well I didn't think you . . ."

"Arthur, this relationship is comfortable. It's nonconfining yet at the same time we know we like each other's company. I hadn't thought of marrying you; so don't feel like you have to ask now that I'm a pity-pat case. I've got to get used to my new eating program. My mind is sometimes spinning on me and the doctor put me on another prescription. I don't know if I like the side effects. Honey, I feel all strung out these days. Don't talk to me about anything I have to think too hard on."

She had her teacher's retirement. When things got too tedious at Cherry Point, he retired early. He knew *he* could live easily on the reduced benefit as long as he supplemented it with fishing and his garden. He had driven with her to the mountains last year and they were planning a trip to Nantucket in the fall. He lightly kissed her good-bye and drove home thinking about what, if anything, had changed between them. His mind returned to thoughts of the children.

Arthur couldn't identify the car in his driveway. The blue and white Cadillac stood in the center of the drive, causing him to have to edge his truck over a hump to get into his garage. As he slammed the door to the truck, he read the front license plate, "Charlotte. Lord 'a mercy, what in the Sam Hill has gotten into Coral to drive down here?"

# Carrot Island

As the girls smeared sunblock on their faces and arms, Jesse helped Meredith load the small boat. When everyone had on a life jacket she pulled the engine's cord. The skiff moved out into the river. Steering a skiff of children with a packed lunch in the floor came naturally for Meredith. She missed the summer days when she could get away from work and join her family on the water. Now that she was going to school, she realized how lucky she had been growing up on the coast. She had classmates who had never headed shrimp or gone clamming. Some became seasick when they went out on the research vessel.

The girls dragged their hands in the water on the way. Jesse cupped his hand and sent a stream of water on both. They screamed their surprise and then started scooping water up to douse him.

"Stop that! Here Jesse, you take my place and steer this. Girls, see if you can see any stingrays in the water." Rachel eased forward and leaned her body against the bow. She rested her chin on her lifejacket and squinted into the water, searching for a large, flat diamond-shaped fish with a long tail swimming above the sandy bottom. Sometimes the water was clear enough to see the bottom. Every now and then, a cloud would pass overhead and all she saw were green ripples as the skiff plowed forward.

Jesse, his eyes seeing all, aimed for the end of Taylor's Creek. Boats were anchored out and swinging wide on their "rode," or anchor line, in the swift current. Dinghies skimmed across to the Beaufort town docks from the anchored and moored boats. Music and voices came across the water. Occasionally he smelled fried seafood or Cajun spices from the many restaurants on the waterfront.

Meredith and Jewel sat on the center seat, scanning the water for signs of sea life. A pair of dolphin jumped in the water beside them. They seemed to be racing them up the creek. They idled past the menhaden plant and the developments being built at the end of Taylor's Creek. A shoal had built up the eastern end of the creek. Jesse throttled down, watching the water depth as he approached the shore.

A new sandbar, on the backside of Carrot Island, had formed a wide, shallow wading pond of blue-green water. They eased ashore there with their bags and blanket. Meredith watched Jesse as he set the anchor up on shore. She let them play a minute then called them over to see her map. "Here, you each have a map and a pad of paper to keep track. Try to stay within the sectors I've marked off. We'll work in pairs, walking the shore and a short distance out. You know what kind of trail horseshoe crabs leave, don't you?" Receiving the affirmative response, they headed out.

Their pads, wet from sweat and water, were filled with hash marks on their return. While they counted horseshoe crabs, they also filled their shelling bags with starfish, Scottish bonnets and sand dollars.

Carrot Island is part of the Rachel Carson Wildlife Sanctuary, home of wild ponies, herons, and numerous other seabirds. Daily tours landed on the other side of the island, an important addition to Beaufort's tourist attractions. People rarely got to the far side of the island where the children were.

As they played in the water, Rachel was careful to lift her arm above her head as she dipped into the cool, gentle waves. Jesse and Jewel dove for shells and lay on the beach in the sun, then sprang up and ran for the water again. Meredith joined in their water fun. She shucked her shorts and shirt from over her swimsuit and dove in with them. While eating their lunch in the afternoon shade of the cedar trees, they talked about the history of the area.

"Rachel, did you know this is where pirates once came and buried their treasure? Blackbeard himself! After his crew helped him to hide it, he killed them all. We might find their bones if we look hard enough. Oh and guess what? There are haunted houses right over there. You gotta get Mr. Arthur to take you on the Beaufort tour bus. There's even one house that has pirate's blood on the floor in the cellar. They tried washing it off and painting it but the stain always comes back! Yo ho ho, me hardies." Jesse chuckled in his fiendish pirate voice. He jumped on the girls but together they bested him and dragged him off into the water.

As they sat in the cool water tossing spray gently at each other, Meredith told them about Rachel Carson, the books she wrote, and how the sanctuary came to be. The breezes were gentle and after the hour wait they headed back to the water, which had changed.

Dark sands blossomed up from the bottom of the water. Jewel reached down, bringing up a handful of the black grit. As she let it slide through her fingers she noticed it left a dark residue on her hands. "Oowah, yuck."

Jesse was quick to note the color change. Dipping his finger into the sand he painted two dark stripes on Rachel's cheeks. "Now you look like a redheaded Indian, Rachel."

"Am not," she pouted, trying to dip her face close to the water to wash it off.

Jewel, always the peacemaker, scooped up another handful of the black stuff and rubbed it on her own arms. "See, we can all be painted!" They plopped down in the inky sand and proceeded to pile the dark mud on their legs and arms. The heat of the sun seemed to vanish under the cool black sand. Meredith sat on the water's edge, dripping the dark coolness over her legs and arms. She noted the change in the tide and called for them to wash off and get things together.

"Hey, this stuff doesn't wash off!" Jesse dove under a ripple of waves to the other side of the sandbar where the water was green. "Maybe the good sand will rub it off. Nope." They rubbed their arms and faces in the surf and still the dark color persisted.

"Well, help me get the things back into the boat and we'll go home to shower," said Meredith.

The children thought their new color was a treat. They began howling like pirates and mocking each other on the ride home. Tourists on the Beaufort waterfront saw a skiff going up the creek with three people on board. The most remarkable of all the creatures was a curly redheaded child with dark face, legs and arms, one in a bright blue cast.

Back at the Garners' home the children begged Meredith to let them take Rachel home. "We'll surprise Mr. Arthur. He'll think pirates or Indians are attacking him." Jesse led the attack. The girls crawled up on Buttercup's back and Jesse pulled his bike from the shed.

Rounding the drive, Rachel hollered back to Meredith, "Thank you for inviting me and for lunch."

Meredith headed for the shower, shaking her head at the hollering and laughing. The pony trotted up the road, topped off with two dark girls shrieking their blood-curdling calls to the myrtle trees and oaks on both sides of the road. Dawg barked running alongside. The invasion of "Austin Paradise" was about to begin.

# Impromptu Calling

Coral immediately began planning her trip after Arthur called to tell her about Rachel's broken arm. "Arthur needs to understand that Rachel will be coming home to me for the rest of the summer. The child is not to be put in further danger," she thought to herself. Purposely, she visited a local sportswear shop to purchase shorts, khaki slacks, and a nautical belt. On a whim she tried on a straw hat and bought that too. She hadn't worn casual clothes in years. Rachel once remarked about her "old lady" look. Coral wore knits, skirts, and dresses like a uniform. She had her hair done each week. Her grandfather had started the mill along the river years before the Depression. The family had always kept up their appearances.

For the first month of summer, she had her obligations, like hosting the book and garden clubs. Commitments behind her, she packed for two days, expecting to pick up Rachel and drive back, stopping at a hotel along the way. She arrived midafternoon at the house. There was no answer when she knocked. The door was open. A big, long-haired cat lifted her head from the porch chair and glared at her. She had come to the house years before when she and Arthur visited during college. She was surprised at the island's growth. She let herself in and walked around the kitchen table. The house was different somehow. She couldn't put her finger on it.

Big pots of cucumbers sat on the kitchen counter. Rachel's paintings hung on the refrigerator and walls. She looked through the ridiculous sunflower curtains and noted the boat was still at the dock. "At least they're not 'at sea!'" She walked into the bathroom and splashed water on her face. She powdered her nose and reapplied her lipstick. She studied her reflection in the mirror. "Not too bad for an old girl."

She had her hair done earlier that week; every golden hair was in place. She liked fixing it herself each morning and wondered how on earth Arthur was dealing with that long red braid of Rachel's. She couldn't help but notice the pictures of her daughter and family, pausing when she saw his wedding band. Two large clamshells nested together on the top of his dresser. They contained loose change, paper clips, and the ring. She picked it up and read the inscription, their names and date of marriage.

Coral smiled, "It might be more proper to have the ring reengraved with the date of our divorce. Oh, he explained why he was leaving. But a man didn't divorce his wife for those reasons in the '60s. Now they don't even need a reason for divorce. People change partners as often as they change cars!

"The nerve of him to leave. He was certainly surprised to find he had fathered a child. There's no mistaking her parentage. She has his eyes, his chin and his stubbornness, or was it my stubbornness?" She could have gone after him, but she didn't. Her pride and her father stopped her. She wondered, "What would have happened if I had followed him back to the coast? Could I have lived here where there are no shopping malls, no book clubs, and no social activities? Why, how could I be happy living where the big event of the week is a high school basketball game, a fishfry or church socials? No, I'm better off in Charlotte where I wouldn't hate him for keeping me here."

She walked back to the porch and studied the garden and the few remaining roses laced through the picket fence. The crepe myrtles nudged the porch railing. The cat didn't lift her head this time. Coral sat in the rocker and relaxed a moment before realizing she was thirsty. She checked the refrigerator for a soft drink. A large pitcher of tea with lemons sat on one shelf near a fish, beer, sandwich meats, bacon and eggs. "At least he's got a well-stocked pantry." She glanced up to see an absurd pink truck pull into the yard. Her fingers clutched the glass as she steadily poured tea over ice cubes watching Arthur come up to the porch. "I was helping myself to your sweet tea, Arthur, dear. Can I pour you some?"

"Afternoon, Coral. No, I think I'm going to have a beer." Arthur took the tea pitcher from her hands and put it back on the top shelf. He grabbed a bottle of his favorite beer. "Care to sit on the porch or would you prefer sitting inside to discuss whatever you had to drive all day to say?"

"As you recall, dear Arthur, first, you hung up on me. Then you call and tell me Rachel broke her arm. Well, the very idea of that child having to endure all that unnecessary discomfort. Since I had it in my head to have Rachel this summer, I decided we could resolve this situation. I'm already here, so I can take her back when we do." She said it all in one breath like a schoolgirl.

Arthur stared at her for a moment. Then he opened his beer on the cabinet-mounted bottle opener. He walked to the front door, holding it open. Coral walked through the door and sat in her rocker. He picked up the cat, sat and rested the cat once again in her sleeping position. Roused to wakefulness, Wobbles stepped politely along Arthur's legs and jumped to the porch. She sniffed the air, strolled to a shady spot and stretched—beginning her afternoon bath.

"Rachel is staying with me, Coral. I told you that on the phone. She's down the road with some friends. I expect them along any time now. You can stay the night. I don't mind, but you have to go home without her. You can't do anything to change my mind. She's having a good time here and I think it's good for her."

Seeing it useless to discuss for the moment, Coral sipped her tea. She had closed her eyes, resting her head on the back of the chair, when she heard the first scream. Dust flying, dog barking, pony trotting, the small marauders attacked. The scene could have come out of a John Wayne movie. Arthur rose from his chair and stood his ground on the bottom step of the porch, arms folded across his chest, beer bottle in hand. Jesse circled, and then drove in, spraying shell grit as he swerved his bike to a halt. Dust rose from the road as two girls bounced in on a pony's back. They slid from their sweat-streaked mount's back and hollered their challenge. Arthur was now thinking the boy might make a good commando or a producer for action movies some day.

Rachel suddenly stopped her war cry, recognizing the woman sitting on the porch. "Grandmother." Her hat was hanging by a string around her neck. Her shoulder bag, tied around the pony's neck, was now being dragged through the grass as Buttercup lowered her head to graze. The strap slid down the pony's short-cropped mane. The children were filthy, if not from their body painting then from the bareback ride up the road on a dirty lathered pony. Their own sweat mingled with the previous war paint. Rachel's red curls were matted to her scalp. She stood there not knowing what to do next.

"Looks like you kids had a good time today. Twins, when you're cleaned up I want you to come back and be properly introduced to Rachel's grandmother. I bet you need to go home to get yourselves cleaned up before your mamma comes home. Rachel, go on upstairs. I'm not too sure you're huggable at the moment. Scrub yourself real good and don't come down until you are pink again." He gave her a gentle swat on her bottom and guided her past her speechless grandmother into the house. Before she climbed the first step upstairs, he squeezed her arm and whispered, "It'll be okay, don't worry." He kissed her on the top of her damp red hair.

"Arthur, was that child really my Rachel? What has she done to herself? What happened to her hair? How could you let this happen to the child? If I didn't have a reason to take her from you before, I have one now. Do you think she is some kind of Huck Finn? She's a little girl, a sweet, gentle child. Arthur, we entrusted her into your care. You let this happen to her. You did this on purpose, to embarrass us. How dare you!"

"Drink your tea and settle down, Coral." He sat for a moment until she had finished her tea. "Inside, she's still your Rachel. She's learning to play and to have fun here." He rocked his chair for a while and let her think. Then he went on, choosing his words carefully, "Rachel is growing here, Coral. She's learning to fish and play and be a little girl. She's also learning to make good decisions. She has chores here. She's proud of her accomplishments. We're going to jar us some pickles tonight after supper and you're welcome to watch or join in. I want to show you how to have fun with your grandchild rather than correcting her or praising her for being a good little girl." He planted his feet on the porch and leaned forward. He took her empty glass and went inside. He brought them both back cold bottles of beer. She looked into his eyes and was drawn back to a summer, many years past, when whatever he did was right and she trusted him. After a few minutes' thought, she wiped the mouth of the bottle and took a long deep swallow of the cold bitter beer.

# Surprise, Surprise

Sarah was up early. Dark clouds threatened a torrential rain; she wanted to arrive before Arthur started breakfast. She had taken the sweet dough from the refrigerator before she showered. She toweled off and ran her fingers through her wet hair. She thought of calling Arthur to tell him she was coming to bring breakfast but decided on a surprise visit.

She pulled a new knit top over her head, yanked up a denim skirt, and shoved her feet into her walking shoes—ugly but comfortable. She began to work the dough on the flat board, forming a thick sheet. She preheated the oven and pulled the sugar glaze from the refrigerator. She had it in a syrup dispenser. It poured better at room temperature. She sprinkled cinnamon and sugar over the butter-brushed dough. She gently curled a long roll of dough. Using a string, she sliced individual sweet rolls and placed them on the cooking sheet.

"Arthur Austin, I want to spend more time with you and your granddaughter," she admitted to herself. The dough puffed up in the oven as she dried her hair. She thought how nice it would be to share breakfast with them on this gloomy morning. Star Willis promised she could handle the opening of the shop. Star had started working for her when she was in high school. During college breaks and summers, it was nice knowing she could depend on the girl to watch the store. With two people now working for her, she was able to relax more and think about what she wanted in life.

She slid a spatula under each browned roll and removed it from the sheet. She allowed them to cool a bit on wire racks before she poured the creamy white sugar mixture over them. Letting them cool more for the sugar to set up, she packed a basket of juice, fruit and her favorite ground coffee beans. She placed the sweet rolls in a cardboard box. As she drove she passed Smitty. He bicycled toward her on the road, having passed Arthur's house. She threw up her hand and almost stopped to invite him to join them, but she didn't want to share the man and his grandchild with anyone this morning. She was curious about the big blue car in the driveway. Sarah parked in the road outside and carried the things up to the house.

Sarah entered the screen door without knocking. She saw another woman in Arthur's arms. As they disentangled themselves from each other, Sarah stood blankly watching. Arthur knew immediately his calming gesture to Coral was misinterpreted. Coral had come from his bedroom in tears a moment before, having realized she would be returning to Charlotte alone.

She had enjoyed watching them put up the pickles. She helped Rachel pack the jars tightly, and then poured the hot syrup over each jar, covering every slice of cucumber. She was startled when a jar was knocked onto the floor. The sweet syrup and cucumber slices splattered on her ankles and shoes.

Rachel jumped down from her perch and placed her hands on her hips shouting, "Lord 'a mercy, now don't that just make a preacher cuss?" Realizing her exclamation was not the proper thing to say, she was more embarrassed by the outburst than the mess. They gathered up the broken glass. After mopping the rest of the kitchen floor with hot soapy water, Coral and Arthur wiped off the jars while Rachel prepared for bed. The jars now stood on the kitchen counter, lined up like soldiers to be reviewed at dawn.

Coral clung to the child when she returned for her good night hug. Things might have been different if she had followed Arthur back to his island. They sat on the porch late, sucking on their cold weeping bottles of beer, talking, until it was time for bed. He showered first and made his bed on the couch. She shut the door and dressed for bed. She watched the dark clouds form across the early morning sky until she finally drifted to sleep. She had a slight headache.

Arthur looked from one woman to the other, not quite knowing what to say. Sarah eyed the folded sheets and pillow on the couch. She also noticed the fancy luggage in his bedroom. She felt dowdy in her denim skirt and tee shirt looking at the elegant lady dressed in a silk kimono with matching soft slippers. As early as it was, it looked as if this woman had just had her hair done. Her complexion was perfect. Sarah's browned face was turning red. For the first time in her life, Sarah Styron was unable to think of anything to say.

She slipped out the door, leaving her basket. "I hope you enjoy this."

Arthur followed her out to the car. "I'm not a guilty little boy, Sarah. No, that's not what I mean to say." He stumbled in his explanation.

"I can't talk right now, Arthur, I must get to the shop." Sarah, filled with emotion, started her van and drove off without looking back. Rain hit Arthur on his bare head as he hurried to the porch. He stood watching her van disappear.

Rachel came downstairs and peered into the packages. Wearing her towel apron, she shifted the warm cinnamon rolls onto a platter. "I have to go dress," Coral said, returning to the bedroom. Arthur filled the coffeepot with coffee. Rachel licked her fingers as the coffee dripped into the clear glass pot.

Orange juice was poured when Coral reappeared wearing khaki slacks and plaid blouse. She was rubbing hand cream on her fingers as she took a sip of juice. "Did your friend decide she couldn't stay? I would like to meet her," she added cautiously.

Arthur poured them coffee and looked out into the yard. Puddles were now forming between the conch shells, which lined the walk. Neither the fresh smell of rain, nor the rumbling of the approaching storm improved his appetite. Rachel poured herself a glass of milk and helped herself to a roll.

"Did Miss Sarah bake these, Grandpa? They're good. Why aren't you eating?" The storm moved in, booming great thunder belches. He rose to shut the windows. "Grandmother, can't you stay another day or two? She can, can't she, Grandpa?" Her grandmother took her hand and held it, mindless of the sticky fingers clinging to her own.

"Child, I have to be getting back. As soon as this rain lets up I'll be on my way." She sipped her coffee, leaving a half-eaten bun on her plate. "I'm already packed. See that you enjoy the rest of the summer. I know you'll have fun fishing and playing with your little friends."

Pulled from his reverie, Arthur seconded Rachel's invitation. "Coral, the child is right. Won't you consider staying another day or two to visit with us? I know you'll enjoy it." He wondered what harm there was in having his former wife visit for a few days. Now they shared not only a daughter but also a granddaughter. "Stay awhile, Coral. Rachel and I would like to take you fishing, wouldn't we, Rachel?" He glanced over to the child as she munched her bun with a white sugar-encrusted mouth.

"Oh, yes, stay. We'll catch a big fish and grill it. Oh, please stay." She licked her fingers, a white sugary mustache lining her top lip.

"Rachel, dear, that's a lovely suggestion but I have nothing to wear fishing. I really must be going home. It's a long drive back." She tried to sound sincere.

"No, stay, please. You used to like to fish. After this storm blows over, the water should lie down. Tomorrow'll be perfect for some blue water fishing. Please reconsider." He looked her in the eyes and touched her shoulder, urging her to change her mind. It was a friendly suggestion to get her to forget her current disappointment and non-pressing commitments at home.

Coral looked at her grandchild and nodded, "I'll stay until we can go fishing together. Arthur, you must write down that recipe for pickles. I want Rachel to help me make them sometime at my house."

"You have to go to the consignment shop, Grandmother; they have really neat clothes you can buy for fishing." A thought like that never crossed Coral's mind.

101

# Belle's Solution

"It was an answered prayer, Sarah. Harold talked with Social Services the same week Brenda Lee called home. Lord honey, was I one happy clam. I'd been working all day on a piece of clay for that new restaurant in Morehead City. I felt good about what was shaping up and knew it was going to be a good day. The phone rang and Pammy Lee got it. She hollered that it was her mamma.

"I flew to the phone and explained what happened. I told her I'd send her gas money to come home and straighten this mess out. She got so hot about the whole thing. I had to calm her down so she could call this caseworker we have. Anyway, she's been here a week now, living at home and getting reacquainted with her daughter.

"Harold came over last night, bringing his family for supper. It was a balm to my heart seeing them all there." For the first time in years Belle wore a nicely shaped dress and makeup, although she still wore her sandals. "I decided to go to Beaufort and buy us all clothes to go to court in. They were having an end of summer sale. I love the colors in this. Do you like it?"

Sarah nodded her head. She was barely listening to her friend, but she was glad things were working in her favor. "Belle, that looks lovely on you. Now that I'm not working full time at the shop, maybe we could get out every so often. You know, take in a movie, go shopping, maybe take a trip out of town?" She was already thinking of ways to fill the gap she foresaw in her life. She had to adjust to this recent development and not sulk like a teenager.

"Why, that sounds like a wonderful notion, Sarah. I never gave much thought to those kinds of ideas. I sat the children down last night and told them about my financial planner. Know what they said? They want me to enjoy this money first. Can you believe that? Brenda Lee has moved back in. She's looking at the community college here. She thinks she might like to try cosmetology. Pammy Lee is so excited I can't keep her settled. And look at me, I look like a new woman." At that precise moment Bitsy Parker entered Sarah's shop. She gave Belle a second glance, not recognizing her.

"Morning, Sarah. Why, Belle Nelson, is that you? I had to look twice. You certainly look different! I mean pretty." Bitsy Parker never could curb her tongue.

"Why thank you, Bitsy, and you look mighty pretty yourself this morning." Belle found it easy to dish out a heavy dose of compliments. Bitsy couldn't wait to make her purchases and make a few calls about this discovery.

"Brandy, I want a loaf of that honey bran bread and a dozen chocolate chip cookies. My grandchildren are coming to visit, don't you know?" She turned once more to stare at Belle. She quickly paid for her purchases and left.

"You'll do fine. It's me I'm worried about. I went to the health food store to see if there's something I can take to replace this other stuff the doctor prescribed. Lord, I don't remember what normal feels like anymore." Sarah didn't want to share her discovery with anyone yet. She'd been over the entire image too many times in her head as the days progressed. She was even thinking of calling her daughter to see if she could go visit for a few days.

Waving Belle off to her new activities, Sarah reached for her old coffee mug, but put it back. She poured herself a glass of sugar-free lemonade. She had lost several more pounds and thought she might want to go shopping later in the week. Nothing used to work at cheering her up like a strong dose of shopping.

# Go Fish

The sound lay like a sheet of silk. In the distance, pink-edged cumulous clouds laced the morning sky. The inlet was quiet and the waters to the cape were eerily pleasant.

Rachel dozed on the bench seat while Coral sat in the mate's chair. They went through shallow Barden Inlet around the cape; there were few white caps. On the ocean side gulls gathered in the distance. Arthur set the boat on self-steering and went back to prepare the fishing poles.

He unzipped the canvas bimini that arched over the aft cabin and brought out the cushions where they could sit to fish over the stern. Rachel woke, yawned and rubbed her eyes, standing in the cockpit. Coral removed the sunblock from a canvas bag. "Here Rachel, let me put this all over your face and arms." She began pouring the lotion into her hand.

Coral wore one of Arthur's old shirts over her new slacks. The long sleeves covered her pale arms. Her hair was tucked under her straw hat. She laughed at the sight she must look with the white cream smeared over her nose. "The bridge club should see me now!" she thought. On her feet she wore a pair of canvas shoes they found at the consignment store. One painted toenail was visible through a small hole.

"The blues are stirring themselves into a frenzy," Arthur remarked as they neared the spot beneath the birds.

Fish jumped out of the churning water. He eased the boat to the side of the ripples so that the fishing lines, with their shiny spinners, edged the agitated water.

Rachel leaned over the aft rail. "Grandpa look at all the fish. They're getting away. I got one! Help me, Grandmother." Coral grabbed Rachel's life jacket and held tight. It had become a second skin to the girl since coming to the island. She liked the feel of additional safety as her grandmother held the back strap.

"Rachel, looks like you got a keeper." Arthur helped bring the fish aboard. As the two lines dropped into the water another fish struck. Arthur compared their size to the marks on the cooler where he kept the fish on ice.

They moved out from the shore, leaving their lines still in the water. Later, Arthur changed the tackle to pick up bigger fish. They listened absentmindedly to the VHF radio as they headed into the sun.

"Lord 'a mercy! Grandpa, I got a big fish!" Rachel jumped from her seat and tugged at the huge pole in the rack mounted on the aft rail. Arthur could tell by the way the rod dipped that this was no blue.

Something struck Coral's line. "Aack!" she squealed.

Arthur left the helm to assist and stood by with a gaff as they pulled in the big fish. "Dolphin, we hit a school of dolphin! These fish—not the mammals—provide some of the best eating there is." They reeled until their arms ached. As soon as they dropped the line back in the water, there was another strike.

Rachel screamed in excitement each time a fish hit her line. "I have to admit this is better than driving all day." Coral spun her head about as another fish hit her line. When Arthur had a chance he grabbed the camera and focused on the anglers and their catches. The lines relaxed as the boat finally swung out of the school's path. Both females lay back on the aft cabin's roof and laughed retelling their catching adventure, absorbing the warmth of the day and the moment. Arthur looked at the bleeding fish in the cooler. He would stop at the fish house and have them dressed. He'd have some packed in ice for Coral to take home. He might be able to sell a few. He would certainly have a well-stocked freezer by the end of the day.

Deciding to call it a day, Arthur turned the boat and headed toward home. Cutting back up the outside of Cape Lookout, the boat took the scenic ride home north of Shackleford Banks. Arthur was eyeing the straight line of red markers on his right when he saw the yellow object on the water. Fishermen often lost cushions in the water, especially after a storm.

Leaving the safety of the channel, he eased through the shoaling waters to see more closely. Reaching for the boat hook to snare the cushion, Arthur stopped as he saw a boot float to the surface. He motioned Coral to take Rachel below as he pulled his boat closer to the floating object.

Tar Boy wasn't going to do anymore crabbing. It appeared that he had fallen overboard and his waders filled with water, holding him down. Air in the boots had spun the careless crabber down headfirst. His face still displayed a look of surprise in death. Arthur reached for his VHF microphone. "Coast Guard Group Fort Macon, this is the *Lady Lou.*"

"This is Coast Guard Group Fort Macon, can you switch and answer 22 Alpha?" came the response.

"Roger," he hit the button and immediately was on the right frequency. "Coast Guard Group Fort Macon, this is *Lady Lou*. I am north of Shackleford Island and I've found a body in the water."

The new Coast Guardsman fumbled with the news. His mind went into the impersonal formatted questions that were required on such reports. He knew the recording device would catch all the information his hands couldn't copy down. "Could you give me a description of your vessel, captain? Can you give me the location of your vessel, captain? Captain, what are your registration numbers? What are the weather conditions at your location, captain? How many people onboard your vessel, sir?"

"I am a white 27-foot Albin with blue canvas bimini. NC 8199 B-Bravo A-Alpha. There are three people onboard this boat. I don't want to stand here and listen to your questions all morning." Arthur exhibited his former brusque manner when irritated. "I'm tiring, I have a child on board and one near-hysterical woman."

He then proceeded to give his latitude and longitude, the weather conditions, including the flow of the current, and whom he had found in the water. He gave it in one long flow of information to keep from having to banter back and forth over the airwaves. As he finished he added, "I'll put a white flare in the air when I see the Coast Guard approaching." He double-clicked the microphone.

Arthur went below to face one very white-faced woman clutching one big-eyed child. They had listened to his radio conversation.

Coral suddenly felt lightheaded. Arthur caught her as she fell forward over the galley table. Rachel put both her hands out in front of her and rested her face on the cool tabletop surface. He poured them some Coke, and told

Rachel to watch her grandmother. Arthur went back above to drop an anchor and watch for the Coast Guard.

It was early evening when they finally reached home. Islanders usually keep their VHF radios on during the day like an open phone party line. They heard Arthur's initial call to the Coast Guard. The fish house was crowded when they arrived to have the fish cleaned. Mr. Taylor placed the thick slices in plastic bags and packed a Styrofoam cooler for Coral.

At home, Arthur washed down the boat and fishing gear before coming into the house. Coral lay on the bed and Rachel colored in her book. A glass of tea formed a wet circle on the table. Arthur broiled fish steaks on the grill while steaming corn on the cob. They had ice cream for dessert.

Dumping the remains in the trash, Arthur and Rachel did the dishes. Coral, tired from the day's activities, swept off the porch, then rocked. Already showered, Rachel rocked beside her with her head laid back on the tall chair. Her hands absently stroking Wobbles, her mind going through the day. Arthur came out, stretched his lean body toward the ceiling, and walked out to the garden to pull a few weeds in the moonlight. A whippoorwill called from across the road, as if singing "Taps" to the long day.

# Make Up or Mess Up

Smitty rode into the drive as Coral shut the lid of her trunk. Hesitating for a minute, she reached for Arthur's hand and held it. "Arthur, dear, it *has* been interesting. You take care of our grandchild or I'll come back to haunt you. Rachel, come here and give me a hug and a big kiss." Smitty parked the bicycle against the fence and approached as Coral held the girl at arm's length. She glanced over her one last time. "You take care of your grandpa and stay out of trouble." She almost sounded cross. Biting her lip to keep from crying, she shut the door of the big car and turned on the air conditioner. Glancing back, she lifted a hand to the chubby man and backed from the yard.

As he glanced at the vanishing car, Arthur asked, "Smitty, have you had breakfast? Rachel and I have some warmed-over cinnamon rolls you might like." He opened the screen door for his friend and the girl, taking one more look over his shoulder at the dust rising from the rock road. Smitty helped himself to the remaining coffee and had a pastry in hand before Arthur could turn around.

Rachel looked at her grandfather's friend, exclaiming, "Did you know what we did yesterday?"

"As a matter of fact, I heard you had a bit of excitement yesterday." The sheriff's car had passed him on the other side of the island as he peddled his morning route. He picked up the news on his journey. He wanted to know the total story, but hesitated to ask with the girl present.

"We caught lots of fish, Mr. Smitty! They were beautiful. I'm going to draw them today. The water was so blue and we ate some last night. They were yummy!" Saying nothing about the body, she shifted down from her chair, put her dishes in the sink, and went up the stairs to brush her teeth.

Smitty waited a minute, then leaned over and asked his old friend for the details. Arthur talked as he washed the dishes and left them to drain in the rack. By the time Rachel reappeared with her colors and fresh paper, the talk had turned from the legged to the finned catch. "Is that right? You don't say?" His friend pictured the whole story. He leaned back in his chair and watched the girl begin to draw on the white paper. He was surprised there was no floating yellow object in the dark blue water. He lifted a section of the newspaper and snapped it straight, beginning to study the business section. "Some things never change," he said as he studied the stock quotes.

Arthur was having similar thoughts. Calling the Garners, he asked if he could bring Rachel over for a few hours. He was anxious to see Sarah and wanted to drop Rachel off on his way. Thankfully, Meredith was there for the day. She invited Rachel to come over. Wrapping up several frozen fish steaks, Arthur tossed them in a plastic grocery bag. He saw his friend to the gate and deposited Rachel, her bike, and the fish at his neighbor's.

As he approached Sarah's gift shop he was glad to see Star's car parked to the side. Arthur pushed open the door and watched Sarah waiting on a customer. Perhaps he could persuade Sarah to take a ride with him. "Morning, Star, Sarah."

He liked to watch Sarah's face move as she talked. Her eyes sparkled with excitement as she waved her hands to finish the story. She had bought some new clothes after she began losing weight and the colors flattered her. Sarah finally closed the cash drawer and called back to Star, "Honey, would you watch things for a while? I need to walk down to the Red and White." She pulled Arthur's arm into her own and edged him toward the door. They both spoke at once as they stepped onto the porch. She laughed quietly, looked down and said, "I want to apologize for my rudeness the other day."

Arthur placed his free hand over hers, which was resting on his arm, and squeezed it. "I was afraid you had come to some wrong conclusions. I want you to know that there is no other woman in my life, just you." Without hesitating he added, "I've been thinking. Want to get married?" He bent to kiss her, inhaling the fragrance of her hair. He raised her hand and kissed it. "Do I have to get on my knee?" he chuckled.

Sarah caught the twinkle in his eye, then rested her head on his shoulder. "Really, stop this. We're on Main Street. People will see." She paused. "Frankly, Arthur, I have to say my head took a spin. It felt like I had a wounded seagull in my chest. My heart didn't stop jumping until that afternoon. Don't talk to me about foolishness now. I was afraid I found out a terrible secret of yours. That was Coral, wasn't it? I guess the whole island knows by now your former wife was staying with you these past few days—and then that horrible Tar Boy business. How did Rachel react to the whole situation? I was worried about her."

"Sarah, I spoke with her about it this morning when I went up to wake her. She didn't know the man. It went right through her as another adventure at Grandpa's! Children are quite flexible. It's the grownups that screw things up, present company included. Now that we're engaged, there can be no doubt in your mind of my intentions."

"I don't remember accepting. I'll have to think about it for a bit." They walked down the street, where she purchased sprinkles and silver balls for a birthday cake. He invited her to dinner that night. "I'll bring wine and an answer, but don't get your hopes up!" She walked him to his pink truck and held the door as he started the engine. She flashed him a smile and a wink, then turned and skipped up the steps to her shop. "I don't skip often enough." Sarah hummed to herself the rest of the day.

Another thunderstorm was forming on the northern horizon as Arthur turned into his drive. He thought the clouds would soon be drenching the Neuse and the boaters on the water. As he left his truck he sighed, watching the sheriff's car pull into his drive. Tom Robinson was elected after his daddy retired from the office. For a young man, he had the diplomacy to remain in office. He formed a good department in spite of the heavy politics in local law enforcement appointments. He shook the young man's hand and offered him a glass of tea as they sat on the porch.

The wind rose across the marsh flats, tossing the tops of the roadside cedar trees. Tom asked carefully worded questions, and finally, "Arthur, is there anything else you remember?"

"I dunno, Sheriff, you hear things about a problem at the fish house. I guess that's no secret but the water takes good men and not-so-good men. It's a hard life. After that storm there could have been a rogue wave that tipped his boat. I guess it was his time."

"I heard about the stolen crabs and the incident at the fish house. You see the Davis boys about when you were coming in that day, or anyone else from the island in that vicinity?"

Arthur spoke slowly, "I told the Coast Guard and your man everything I observed that day. To be frank, we'd been up early and it was a long day. I was tired; my family wore me out. The sun, wind, and water works on you after a while. If someone else was around there I didn't see them."

The sheriff rested his empty glass on the porch railing and stood up. "Thank you for your answers and the tea, Arthur." Tom Robinson walked back to his car.

Arthur wondered as the man drove off if, in fact, someone had helped Tar Boy to flip into the water.

He shook his head, scooped up the glasses, and went in to change into old clothes to do a bit of weeding before the rain came. Weeding always helped to put things in perspective and run off a bit of energy. He never thought asking Sarah to marry him would cause the emotions he was feeling now. It seemed natural and the perfect answer to him at the time. He could kick himself for not going to the trouble of doing it right—on bended knee, and he didn't have a ring for her. Rachel came home in time for a late lunch. They made peanut butter sandwiches and drank tall glasses of milk while the storm pounded on the tin roof. She was tired from her play and decided to take a nap.

Arthur pulled out a rule and pencil and began taking measurements of his house.

# YES

When Sarah arrived, she and Arthur rocked on the porch, inhaling the damp air and sweet marsh fragrance. "It's been an interesting summer." Sarah swung around in her chair as she heard Rachel coming down the steps inside. "Well, Rachel, come here—I have something to tell you." Rachel came out the screen door. "I told you you'd be the first person I'd tell. Today your grandpa asked me to marry him. What do you think I should do?" Sarah grinned over Rachel's head into Arthur's face.

"Are you serious? Awesome, Grandpa!" She hopped onto his neck and gave him a big smooch. Then she did the same to Sarah. "I think that's perfect. How did he ask you? When will you do it? Can I come? Gosh, tell me everything." Rachel finally stopped.

"Whoa, whoa, settle down a bit." Arthur, more in control now, took a deep breath. "She hasn't told me yes yet." He paused, waiting.

Sarah hugged Rachel in her arms, resting her head on top of the girl's. "Hmmm. I think I'd like to be married again, Arthur, unless you want to take that question back." Rachel swiveled her head back to see her grandfather.

"Nope, I'm sure. It's a done deal. Now if that's settled, we can go in and start supper." Arthur rose from his rocker and went to take the sketches he had worked on all afternoon off the table. "Take a look at these while I get everything out." He handed Sarah and Rachel plans for enlarging the house to include a bigger kitchen, master bedroom, den, and a porch around the entire house, including a screened portion on the back. Rachel hopped in through the door, slapped her grandpa a high five with her good arm, and nodded approvingly. She washed her hands, tucked in her apron and proceeded to set the table.

Out on the porch Sarah redrew a few lines, sketching in a few things to include a walk-in closet and larger pantry. She then rose to join the meal preparations. She washed the fresh green beans in a colander. "I think the plans are good, very good, and when we finish eating dinner we'll go over them together." Arthur nodded and took the basket of shrimp, scallops, and green and red peppers out to his grill.

After supper they sat at the table. "Now let's get a few things settled." Sarah took a new notebook from her purse and began making a list. "Okay, first, we talk about the house arrangements. I agree we're going to live here after a few changes are made. I can rent out my apartment and the income will go toward your renovations. Don't say a word, Arthur, this will be my house, too, and I plan to put some money into it. Never had a kitchen or a bedroom I was ever happy with. I want us to do this one right." Arthur sat tight-lipped, resting his arm on her chair back. "Now, Rachel, you had a part in him asking me the big question, not that I was ever looking for it, mind you, so I won't get married without you."

Rachel nodded her head emphatically, "Good. I'm coming back next summer, aren't I Grandpa? Can we do it then?"

Arthur scratched his chin, "Reckon we can talk to your folks and see what they say. I hope you'll want to come back every summer, Picklepuss."

"I'm not Picklepuss, Grandpa, that's my doll." She enjoyed his nickname for her but still liked to chide him.

"Alright, back to decisions at hand." Sarah made a few notes on her pad. Together they went over the plans and measurements. "Arthur, when will all these house renovations be done? Can it be finished by next summer? I always thought being a June bride might be a little exciting. Wait 'til I tell my children. You know everyone will want to be here, that includes a good portion of the population of this island!"

"Hmmm," Arthur grunted. Shifting in his chair, he said, "Would anyone like something to drink?" Going to the refrigerator, he removed two bottles of beer and poured a glass of tea for Rachel. "This planning stuff can make a person very thirsty."

"I'm going to make a list of who we want to invite. Also, Rachel, what do you like to eat at weddings? There's also flowers—and how big a wedding do you want dear, just family or the works?" The plans continued until late evening when Rachel went to bed.

# Day on the Shore

Several families were together net fishing and clamming, including Arthur, Sarah and Rachel. Extra hands were welcome when it came to stretching a long net out over the water, then pulling it in from shore. Fish flopped on the wet sand as they were separated. The smaller ones were thrown back in the water. Larger ones were gutted and put on ice for later. Grills were set up for cooking.

Earlier that day, young and old crawled on hands and knees in the cool water, feeling for the small cherrystone clams. Adults stood waist-deep in the water, digging down with their toes. When they felt a clam, they would squat and bring it up. Children crawled through the water on all fours, digging into the sand with their fingers. The pile of clams grew until they were divided into several pots, along with corn on the cob, hot dogs, chicken, yams, Irish potatoes, shrimp, and water. When it came to clambakes and fish grilling on the beach, no one went home hungry.

They spread the food on pieces of plywood held up by coolers or folding tables brought from home. Children sat in the sand with plates loaded with corn, hot dogs, and their choice of seafood. Rachel enjoyed the tender clams as she dipped them into the squeezed butter and dropped them onto her tongue. They were chewy and good. Her grandfather had mixed up a ketchup-based horseradish sauce that made her sneeze. Her hands and face were smeared with sweet kernels of corn and dripping butter. She grabbed a paper towel and wiped her mouth.

The bony fish were more appealing to the older ones in the group. She watched with curiosity when a wrinkled-faced woman bit into a non-filleted fish. Her toothless gums easily pulled the meat free from the backbone.

"Moighty fine eating, y'all." Bitsy Parker held the huge pot up to scoop more food into the bowls on the table. "There's more where that come from. Pot liquor anyone?"

Sarah leaned back in her beach chair. "Arthur, I'm full as a tick," she said, crinkling her nose with pleasure. Misplaced hair stuck out from under the brim of her large hat. Sarah and Arthur had gone to Stampers in Beaufort and picked out the sapphire-and-diamond engagement ring she wore on her left hand.

"Rachel, honey, would you go get me one of those black walnut and cranberry cookies I brought? They're in the blue box on the table."

Rachel rose, carrying their plates to the large black trash bag tied to the back of one of the tables. She dropped the plates into the bag, then scampered over to see what the other children were doing. She came back in a roundabout way, finally clutching a handful of cookies on new napkins, one already in her mouth. "Theeth are gooo," she garbled through a mouthful of cookie. She reached down to take a sip of her drink. "Grandpa, I don't want to go home yet. I'm as full as a tick too, Miss Sarah."

"Honey, you watch you don't pick up too many of the things I say. Your folks in Charlotte might not enjoy my expressions." She winked at the child and inhaled the black walnut flavor of the cookies as she took a bite. "I think like you, child. This day could go on forever."

Billy Taylor lumbered by. "Come, sit for a while, Billy. Where's the rest of your family?" Arthur moved a bit closer to Sarah on their sand knob.

"Afternoon, Arthur, Sarah. Oi guess you heard they held the inquest for Tar Boy the week a' fore last. Had some kind of fancy name, like 'Miss Adventure' or some sech. You reckon anybody did do him in?" The three adults gazed out over the water, shaking their heads. "Arthur, Oi heard you and the youngun found him, that right?" Left alone in the fish house, Billy had a way of making his fish talk when he wanted a conversation.

"Billy, let's let that story go," Arthur responded. "Tell me about all that excitement from the other night. I must have heard sirens going off all over the island."

"Yes sir, Oi reckon it was about 10:30 when Oi first heard that screaming machine and then about twenty minutes later I he'ard another on' further down the road. That feller must have got a dozen radios and disc players before he hit the first locked car. When he broke into a locked car, you see, the alarm went off. If it were me doing the stealing, I'da come by boat.

"That's what done him in. Yes, sir. The fool should have known this island has a foolproof burglar system. Little missy," now looking at Rachel he explained, "them folks called the bridge tender, you see? They told him what happened and the bridge tender jest lifted that ol' draw. Didn't take long for them to get our sheriff's deputy outta bed. Some inlander, humph. They found him sitting, dumb fool, in his vehicle waiting for the draw to close. Right there at the gate, can you imagine that? He never knew'd what happened when the deputy tapped on his window and asked him what for. That boy didn't even have time to hide the stolen stuff under the seat." Billy shifted in the sand and stood up. "Lord, honey, these bones can't sit too long. Oi better get on down yonder and see what other kind of trouble Oi can get into." He tipped his greasy, brimmed hat as he straightened and wandered down to the shore.

"Well, that was enlightening. I have more news," Sarah smoothed the towel across her lap and began. "A new set of twins was born this week. They're pretty sure there is another set on the way for the Lewis family. I've heard comments made about this island water being the cause. There's also a petition. I'd like for you to consider signing it, Arthur. It's to ban jet skis from the island's water. They're such nuisances." She got out her notebook from the beach bag she was carrying. "Do you want to go to the church supper this Wednesday night? I could make a big pan of lasagna." Church socials were the norm for Wednesday nights.

"I don't know how I've got along without you and that notebook, my love. Rachel, do we have plans for this Wednesday?" Arthur gathered their cups and napkins as he rose to his feet, stretching. Red curls nodded "no," then jumped again to take the trash from her grandfather and help Sarah up.

They packed their belongings back into the boat and waded back to say thanks and promise to do it again. Arthur had to line up the streetlights going up his channel, finding his way home after dark. He helped Sarah take her things to her van while Rachel towed her satchel into the house. She didn't bring Picklepuss along anymore.

"You sure you want to go back to your place tonight?" Arthur hinted under his breath. "It's been a long summer so far, my sweet." He held Sarah close, smelling the heat and saltiness of her body.

"Arthur, you know better. Besides, Rachel's here." She ran her hand down his cheek. His beard was already rough from a day's growth, but she liked to feel it. He kissed her and held the door open as she shifted into her seat and buckled up. "Will I see you tomorrow?" she asked.

"Don't be surprised." Arthur walked behind the house, noting the upstairs light was already turned out. He stepped off the dock, down to the boat. After washing the boat down, he re-coiled the hose and headed for the house. Taking a deep breath, he climbed the front porch steps. "It's gotten to be a long summer, down east on Nelson Island thanks to you, Picklepuss." He sat on the porch for a while before going inside.

# Hurricane Beverly

"Hold this box of screws for me, Rachel. Hand me them one at a time." He was putting precut plywood sheets on the front of Sarah's store windows.

"Okay, Grandpa." Rachel balanced the box of screws and handed Arthur another screw as he finished drilling one edge with his cordless tool. "What will the hurricane do here? I've never seen one."

"Well, I don't think this'll be a bad one. If it gets any bigger we might have to leave the island but I've been through a lot worse here since I was a boy. There'll be a lot of wind and rain. That's why we have to board the windows up and put everything inside so it doesn't get blown around or broken." During the preceding weeks, hurricane season had officially opened with little effect on the community or North Carolina's coast. An early depression had become a tropical storm and, finally, a hurricane in the past week. "All indications project the hurricane to hit the Outer Banks about eighty miles from here."

Sarah came out of the shop. "Does anyone have any special requests for supper tonight? Arthur, do we have enough water and bread? How about candles, batteries?"

"Lord, Sarah, it's not like we're going to be without for a month. Between what I have at the house and what you have in your freezer, I can't think of a thing we need. What do you think Picklepuss? Do we need anything?"

"I dunno," Rachel shrugged her shoulders.

"Well, I'm making one more trip to the store. I'll meet you two later at the house. You take care, now." Sarah locked the front door and hurried to her van as the wind began gusting.

✿ ✿ ✿

Later at Arthur's house, "Rachel, can you pull that line and bucket in the shed for me?" Arthur was setting out his kedge anchor to hold *Lady Lou* off the dock. He rowed his skiff over to the marsh and waded into the reeds to place the anchor.

Overhead, the sky alternated between clear calmness and drizzly blowing winds as the storm moved nearer. Taking one last look about the yard, they entered the house. Stepping around the porch rockers, which had been dragged inside, Rachel dashed to answer the phone.

"Oh, hello, Grandmother. Yes, we're fine. My arm? No, I don't even use the sling anymore. I use my hand like nothing's wrong with my arm. Uh huh, I mean, yes ma'am. You want to talk to Grandpa? Okay, he's right here." Rachel held out the phone for her grandfather.

"Good morning, Coral. No, we've been away most the morning and I don't have an answering machine. No, we plan on staying here. It's a category two storm now. It'll probably drop once it hits land. No, we'll be fine. Don't worry. Yes, I'll have Rachel call you as soon as it goes by. If the lines are down it may take a day.

"No, I don't get cable. I can't see the Weather Channel. You'll probably see more of the storm than us . . . Then you stay tuned in and let us know. I have a radio here at the house and a boat radio, the VHF. We'll keep up with the marine forecasts. The winds and our barometer will let us know when it passes us." He administered to Coral's anxiety, then hung up. "Humph, hadn't talked to that woman in thirty-some years, Picklepuss. You show up and we're old friends again." He talked to the doll as he picked it up off the sofa and sat down for a minute, resting.

Rachel came down from her room. Arthur asked, "Are your windows closed? It will hit us first from that side of the house before she passes. When the eye is above us, it will come from this other side by the kitchen."

"How do you know that, Grandpa?" Rachel took the doll from his hands and sat beside him.

"Well, these ol' storms rotate counterclockwise while they travel, see?" He drew a swirl on her tablet of paper. "Coming like they predict, the center of the storm will pass here and that means these winds will be like this. And as it moves up the coast, then it reverses. See how the winds move from the other side?"

"Wow." Looking up from the drawing, Rachel saw Sarah pull into the yard. "Miss Sarah's here." They went out to meet her.

"I've pulled my truck over to the wall in the garage, Sarah. You drive in there beside it. Both vehicles will be out of the storm." As Sarah parked and gathered her things, he continued, "Yes sir, when my granddaddy bought this property from the church he knew this was some of the highest land on the island. See, this is where the old church used to be. That's why we have the cemetery as a neighbor. He started building this house when my daddy was born and it's been added onto ever since." Helping Sarah with her suitcase and groceries, he added, "and will still be added on, Lord willing." He winked at Sarah as they carried the packages into the house. The rain had started again. Arthur stood on the porch a while, watching the storm approach.

"Usually it comes during the night. I bet this one is the first one we've had in fifty years to hit in the afternoon." Sarah pulled off her rain jacket and began loading the refrigerator. "Honey, help your grandfather put new batteries in all these flashlights. Arthur, where is the lantern?"

"Forgot to bring it in. With all these candles and flashlights, we might not even need it. By tomorrow night we should have power. Everything should be pretty much back to order. Well, what do you want for an afternoon snack? Anyone up for popcorn and Monopoly?" He reached for the board game and turned on the radio sitting on the kitchen counter.

"I am, I am," Rachel opened the board and picked her favorite piece, the silver hat.

Sarah poured oil and popcorn into a large pot, then placed the pitcher of iced tea on the table. "You pour dear, I have to put something else on my list of things to do." Two hours later the wind was howling outside. They lost power about the same time, and lit the candles.

"Is it okay for me to go to the bathroom?" Rachel asked. Receiving the affirmative, she went upstairs. A moment later, she yelled down, "Grandpa, rain is coming in my windows. Lord 'a mercy. What a mess!"

Grabbing towels from the linen closet and a large pot, both adults rushed upwards. "There, that should do it. We'll check up here more often. Here, squeeze that towel into the pot, Arthur." Sarah sopped up the sill and stuffed another towel around the leak. "Let's look around and see if there're anymore leaks."

"Yuck, my knapsack is all wet." Rachel found another leak in her closet.

"I've been meaning to re-caulk around the chimney. This closet backs up right against it. Well, Sarah, add that to our contractor's list. Are we supposed to meet with him sometime next month after Rachel leaves?" To Rachel he said, "We thought after you leave it would be easier to tear out a few walls and add a few spaces. Okay, Picklepuss?"

"Fine with me as long as I have my room when I come back. Come on y'all. Let's go finish the game," she grinned, hoping it meant she could stay up very late. After fresh tuna fish sandwiches, the three sat in the living room as the storm boomed outside. Windows rattled and occasionally the screen door slapped against its hook. Wobbles purred in Rachel's lap as they listened to reports on the local radio station, which was relaying caller's information to its listeners. It was surprising how cell phones increased the number of call-ins.

"Arthur, it would be nice to have gas logs on that wall, don't you think?" Sarah got out her notebook as Arthur considered that option. "It'll be cozier in the winter and probably cut down on our heating bills."

"You know that will be . . ." the wind outside had dropped to a whimper. "Let me peek outside for a minute. Rachel, that means the eye is passing us. Sarah, grab that big torch flashlight. Let's see if Wobbles wants to go out for a minute." He lifted the cat up to take her out.

Arthur, Sarah, and Rachel stood on the porch staring into the evening, stilled momentarily. Not a creature chirped from the marsh. The cat stretched briskly and jumped to the ground, picking her way through the puddles. "Oh, look at the garden and the fence." In the darkness the garden, pelted by the storm, was miserable. Even the sturdy okra and tomato bushes were on the ground. A section of the picket fence had blown into the road. The water had risen halfway up into the yard from the marsh.

"I'm going to run out there and pick up the fence section. Then I'm going to make sure all the lines on the boat are holding. Now the winds are going to be blowing her off the dock." Arthur reached for his rubber boots and sat on the porch edge, pulling them on.

Sarah noted that Wobbles had returned from her venture, shaking her fur. "You better hurry, this cat knows when to come in out of that storm." She and the girl watched Arthur pull the fence section back into the yard and push it under the porch. He went around to the back. They followed, watching him through the windows. "Let's go upstairs again and wring out those towels. It shouldn't leak so badly up there now. It'll be the kitchen window we have to check next." Peering out of the top window, they noticed Arthur tying the propane gas tank back in place. He wedged a cinder block against it and went to his toolshed. "I hope he hurries; I don't want him to be caught out there when the wind starts back up."

As she spoke, the front door slammed shut in the wind. Rain pelted the front of the house. Sarah ran downstairs and held the large torch light, shining it out through the double glass window for Arthur to work.

"Finally! That storm all but sucked the air out of my lungs." He slipped the boots from his feet and carried them to the sink.

"Well, it's about bedtime for you young lady, want to camp out on the floor? Go pull all those blankets off the cedar chest and we'll set up camp right here. Here's a pitcher of water. Use that to brush your teeth and drink. This is why we filled all these jugs with water, Rachel. We don't know if the water is contaminated that we get from the sink now. And if we get a busted water line we'll use this other to flush the toilets. As long as they flush on their own, we won't use what we saved in the tubs."

Rachel crawled between the sheets. While Sarah tucked her in, Arthur rose to tap the barometer. "Well, it's been six hours now since we first felt her. Miss Beverly is moving on out. Get some sleep Rachel; there'll be a lot of work tomorrow."

Exhausted, Rachel went to sleep listening to the rain assaulting the east side of the house.

# Morning After

"The island bridge is closed as a precautionary measure. Looters sometimes take advantage of empty houses following a storm. The local deputy checks identification before allowing anyone back. Most of the residents living too close to the water have spent the night in the Nelson Island Middle School, sleeping on cots in the gymnasium." Arthur talked as Sarah drove.

"Lord 'a mercy, Arthur, look—the bell has been blown out of the church tower." Sarah stopped, along with other drivers, to stare at the damage. "That'll take a few bake sales and suppers to repair. Uh-oh, they are turning us back, must be a line down up there."

Rachel could see a bucket truck up ahead. "Grandpa, is that why we don't have power or telephones?" Sarah took another turn, determined to get to her store. "Oh, my gosh, Miss Sarah, look, there's your sign." Someone had propped the sign up against the corner stop sign.

"Look's like a good advertisement, Sarah. You can read it like, Stop, for Sarah's Bakery and Gifts." Arthur climbed out of the van and lifted the sign into the back. Proceeding cautiously, they finally reached her store.

"Well, thank the Lord. Everything looks alright." Sarah parked the vehicle on the street and walked around her building checking for damage. "Come on. Let's go inside to see if it leaked much. Humph, one of the vents must have blown crooked. Would you look at this mess? Water dripped from the ceiling around my ovens. Arthur, would you mind climbing up there and seeing if it looks bad? We'll have to tarp it down until I can get someone to fix it."

"If this is going to be a real partnership, I'm pulling rank here." He went to the van and pulled out his toolbox. "Picklepuss, mind the store while Sarah and I check out the roof." Rachel wandered into the kitchen and shop. Everything was draped with plastic. Flashlight in hand, she stepped over puddles inside the store. Finally, she heard footsteps and knocking above.

Sarah returned. "I'm going to run back to the house for some caulking while he finishes up. You want to come or stay?" Sarah grabbed up her purse; Rachel followed her out.

"I think I'll stay here in case Grandpa needs me." Rachel backed into the street trying to see the man working on the roof. Having no luck, she saw her friends riding their bikes toward her.

"Rachel you ought'a come see our barn. Roof completely blew off. That ol' wind rolled her right up and dumped it in our front yard as pretty as you please. Oh, the animals are fine, they got a little wet, but all the hay may have to be thrown away. How did you all make out?" Looking up at the noise overhead, he asked, "Hi, Mr. Arthur, need a hand?" Jesse rolled his bike up on the sidewalk; Jewel followed. "More gawkers out today than I've ever seen. Guess with a day off from work there'll be a lot of looking as folks drive about." He picked up a stone and threw it at a tree. The children sat on the damp curb.

Jewel pulled on Rachel's arm. "Look, a rainbow. It sure is pretty." The bright morning light streamed through the mist, leaving the multicolored signature. "Were you afraid, Rachel? You've never been in a storm like this, have you?"

Elbow on her knee, Rachel thought about the question a moment. "You know, I never had a chance to be afraid. There was too much going on. It was exciting, sorta, and fun. We camped on the floor." The children drew figures in the dirt edging the road.

"When do you have to go home, Rachel? Are you staying until the end of the month? I'm going to miss you." Jewel enjoyed her new friend. "Our school starts before Labor Day, the last week in August. I'll write to you if you want."

"Yeah, I'll miss you guys too. And I'll write you both back. Do you have an e-mail address? That will be fun. Umm, my school starts later than yours, but Mamma and Daddy are coming on the twentieth to pick me up." Rachel looked up to see Sarah return. The twins rode off on their bikes as Arthur came down from the roof.

"Well, that takes care of that. Let's get home and start cleanup there." Arthur placed his toolbox in the van and they rode back home.

"Now the real work begins." Sarah and Arthur, pulling on work gloves, reached for rakes. "We've got to clean up this mess. Watch where you step. Rachel, honey, run inside and get those big leaf bags I bought. Then, why don't you pick up the bottles, cans, and small boards while we try to rake up this mess? Here, take this other pair of gloves."

The high tide from the sound had dumped a line of marsh reeds, shore trash, pieces of docks and boats. Rachel picked her way through the backyard, collecting cans and bottles. They worked past lunch before they finished. "Twenty-one, twenty-two bags, Grandpa. That's a lot of trash." She carried the last bag to the curb. "I wasn't sure what to do with these. Tell me if these bottles are special before I throw them away."

Going to the porch, Rachel picked up a handful of glass bottles. "See, they're different colors, green, some sorta purple. Some are clear."

"Ho hoa! Rachel, these are old-time medicine bottles. The storm must have loosened up someone's old stash. They used to sell something called laudanum, made from opium. Some people became addicted to it and tried to hide their habit. There was a lady in Beaufort who used to drink the stuff and throw the empties under her porch. I think when they excavated her house back in the 1960s they found thousands of bottles there. When I was a boy these sold for about two dollars each. You can keep them or probably sell them at the antique store." Arthur held the bottles to the sun noting the old glass color.

"Time for lunch, or supper, whatever you call it. I vote for oyster stew. How does that sound? Arthur, you have some oysters thawing in your freezer. I'm going to start heating the milk. Hook up the propane, will you?" Arthur had disconnected the tanks during the storm. They breakfasted on cereal, making coffee on his grill.

"How you all doing?" Smitty rode into the yard. "I'm not interrupting anything am I?"

"No, Smitty, your timing is excellent. Sarah is starting some oyster stew. Care to join us?" Arthur helped the man pull his bike up through the pools of standing water.

Smitty rubbed his hands together and pulled up his pants, "Don't mind if I do. Nope, don't mind if I do. Thank you for inviting me."

# Vacation Bible School

Both Arthur and Sarah were hugging their sides. In fact, the whole room was chuckling, trying hard not to laugh. Each year at the conclusion of the children's Vacation Bible School all the participants and teachers put on a play. After attending weekly services with her grandfather, Rachel joined the youngsters in the summer's final production, *Jonah and the Whale*.

It turned comedic when some little fishies in the sea had turned on each other. They tussled back and forth while the main characters tried to remember their lines in spite of the commotion their fellow thespians created. Usually the play producer only worried about forgotten lines, misplaced scratching hands, or nose picking. This year's play had people standing in the back in order to follow the entire performance, planned and otherwise. Their songs, dances, and dialogue had every member of the audience on the edge of their seats, if they were still sitting. In one of the last scenes a palm tree and worm had toppled over on the desert and begun kicking each other, much to the director's dismay. The applause and cheers at the play's conclusion were beyond expectation. Parents, grandparents, and well-wishers pushed forward to hug the performers and congratulate the production staff. Ice cream, cookies and lemonade were served in the church parlor.

"Well, I thought that went rather well," grinned Smitty as he hitched up his trousers. Because his daughter was nowhere in sight, he took a double scoop of ice cream and topped it with chocolate syrup. His grandson was one of the kicking children during the last scene.

"I think what you mean is that it was unforgettable." Arthur shook hands with the minister and Barbara Moore, the director of children's programs. He saw neighbors and friends he hadn't seen all summer. He never realized that keeping a child busy for a couple of months would keep him out of his familiar routine—that now seemed monotonous.

Arthur now had more patience than he used to have with people, and children especially. He was more aware of his appearance and how he spoke. He was engaged to a woman that he should have married a long time ago. He hadn't worked this hard at planning and detail since he retired. He was actually looking forward to doing it again, and next summer, there was going to be a wedding.

"Rachel, you were an adorable king's aide." Sarah hugged her to her side. Rachel quickly pulled off her robe, in spite of her cast, and piled it in the large box of costumes. She hopped on one foot and scratched her leg, looking around for her new friends. During the preceding week mothers and other volunteers dutifully showed up each morning providing games, Bible stories, snacks, and cleanup. He never knew so much work went into the yearly production. His involvement had been minimal in years past.

"Arthur, I hope I can count on your carpentry skills again at Christmas this year." Barbara Moore's voice reached out to him above the noise of the crowd. "You certainly have a knack for scenery design."

"Yes, he has very good designing ideas," smiled Sarah as she pulled him away from the aggressive woman. To Arthur she added, "I'm going to have to keep my eyes on you, young man. I understand you spent a lot of time up here working on the set. Whoever painted the inside of that whale's belly knew what they were doing."

"Oh, you're jealous because they didn't ask you to help with the refreshments tonight." He squeezed her hand and looked about for Rachel. He excused them away from the crowd at the table and found his way back to the coat rack.

The evening foretold another storm and he wanted to be on his way before the first drops. "Rachel, are you ready to go?" He finally got her attention and signaled for her to get her rain jacket. Huge drops of rain were already hitting the grass as they hurried to his truck.

"I'm sorry now I didn't let you drive, Sarah." He flipped up the top but there remained a half-inch gash between the cut metal edges of the cab top and windshield, where it had been severed years before. During the winter months he duct taped the edges closed, but during the summer he put up with the inconvenience. As he drove Sarah home, puddles formed on the roof, plunging into their laps every time they slowed or stopped.

Rachel squealed in delight as the cold water splashed down. "It's only water. I'm afraid this is one of those times I wished I had a regular car. Sorry for the bath we're getting," Arthur apologized again.

"Nonsense, dear." Sarah slid over closer to him in the wet seat. "I wouldn't have it any other way." When he stopped at her shop another sheet of water cascaded into the cab. He watched her as she climbed up the side steps to her home. Then, putting the Pink Panther in gear, he drove away.

Rachel was ecstatic with the water splashing down outside and inside. "Does this mean I don't have to take a bath tonight?" she giggled holding her damaged arm close to her chest. Her damp hair was already getting some length back to it since the day of its demise.

"No, young lady, you will take a hot shower, towel off good, and hop into bed." He drove the truck under the cover and they both dashed to the house.

# Go Chase a Cloud

It was Rachel's last full day with him. Arthur was expecting company. His daughter and her husband would be coming later in the day. Rachel held his hand as they walked the shoreline at Atlantic Beach. Occasionally they stopped to more closely examine a shell or jellied body of sea life as it wavered in the tidal foam. The child dropped her grandfather's hand. "I'm afraid Mamma won't like my hair or my new clothes," she pouted.

The brisk wind was out of the north and the dunes formed cliffs along the beach. Strands of sea grass drew semicircles in the sand. The beach was littered with old tires, driftwood, and the regular sea trash thrown up by the previous high tide. Occasionally a bird screamed over their heads. The waves broke short, dark blue fingers along the shoreline, a reminder of the violent storm of the preceding night. The sun had been up barely an hour, and already the fishing pier in the distance held several pole-bearing anglers hoping to catch the last fleeing fish before they were sucked back into the depths with the tide.

"Might not, but then, she'll be so happy to see you she probably won't even notice." He wore a yellow slicker and rolled-up jeans. Rachel chased the seagulls and sandpipers among the surf waves. She held her encased arm above her head as she ran. She returned, gleefully tugging on his hand to go faster, her energy more vigorous than his.

She screwed up her face and asked, "You think so? I bet she didn't miss me. I missed her at first, but, Grandpa, we had so much fun I forgot I missed her."

Rachel, oblivious to the chill, threw off the sweatshirt hood from her head and twirled in circles, giggling. When she became dizzy she plopped down on the moist sand. Arthur quickly yanked her up and spanked off the wet sand that clung to her faded jean bottom. He smiled down at her glowing face and growing red curls. "Young lady, I believe you've grown a foot since you've been here, and with this curly short hair, I'm mighty pleased with you. I think she'll like what she sees." Already the consignment store clothes seemed a part of her. Her hair blew helter-skelter in the morning breeze. "What did you like most about this summer, Picklepuss?" he asked.

"Well I liked driving the boat and learning about how to tie knots and stuff. I even liked having to clean my room and helping you fix breakfast. I have new friends—Jewel and Jesse and Pammy Lee. I had fun decorating your living room. I really liked visiting Miss Belle and doing all the art projects. I want to make pickles again next year, okay?" Rachel paused with her memories. "I liked cooking shrimp and better—eating them! Did Grandmother already tell her about my arm, the haircut, and everything? I'm still worried."

"They'll be here about suppertime, Rachel. We still have today. I want you to remember your manners now." Arthur spoke as if he had rehearsed his speech. "You go on back to your grandmother's. I don't want to hear back that you lost your manners.

"You'll go back to sitting properly like a young lady in your plaid jumpers or flowered smocks." Arthur groaned to himself as he continued his lecture. "You don't forget about us here on the island. Sarah and me expect you back here next summer . . ."

They ate breakfast at the fishing pier grill. Arthur wasn't as hungry as he thought he would be. "Grandfather, what'll we do after breakfast?" she queried, reverting back to calling him what she called him that first evening they met. Rachel was also feeling the significance of the day. He smiled, scratched the few remaining hairs on his head, and looked out at the water and sand.

"Let's go chase those clouds by the lighthouse," Arthur grinned and slid the chair back beneath the table as Rachel ran for the door. "We'll worry about later when it gets here."

Together man and child walked back down the beach to the pink truck.